A MAP OF MURDER

A SEABREEZE BOOKSHOP COZY MYSTERY BOOK 6

PENNY BROOKE

CHAPTER ONE

*E*loise Endicott was late to work the plant booth at the Merchants Guild Spring Fling.

"I'm thinking she forgot, Rue," said Paul Budd as he neatened the brochures on local gardens and the county garden club. He said it nonchalantly, but I could see the look of concern move across his intense green eyes. Those eyes and his dark good looks were the reasons Paul was the most sought-after bachelor in Somerset Harbor, Massachusetts. That was our little piece of white-sand paradise, not far from Cape Cod.

Now he glanced down at his stylish watch with the blue, expensive-looking face. He was due any minute, I supposed, at one of the upscale smoothie shops he owned. But, of course, he couldn't leave without Eloise to relieve him at the table filled with yellow and purple blooms and lush-looking plants local gardeners had donated to the festival. Proceeds would be going to the charities supported by the merchants guild.

"Let me just run to her shop real quick and check," I said, telling myself all was well. Eloise was somewhere in her seventies but seemed to be in fine health, even taking what she referred to as her "beauty walks" around the downtown streets almost every day. Paul probably had it right, that she had just forgotten this change to her routine. I had seen her mind slip just the slightest bit over the past year—a name forgotten here or there, an item meant to be shipped to a customer but left waiting on the shelves.

"Back in just a minute. Hopefully with Eloise," I said. But the problem was my dog seemed to have other plans for where we were going next. Gatsby threw his nose high up in the air, picking up the smell of hot dogs, barbecue, and a myriad of other foods being handed out in cardboard trays in the food tents to my left. I scratched behind the soft ears of my golden retriever and best buddy. "Let's go find Eloise, okay? Then later we'll find treats."

Something of a tug-of-war ensued as I headed right and Gatsby made a mighty effort to move us in the direction of the food extravaganza, which I did admit smelled tempting with its aromas of grilled meat and an array of spices. I would be back for sure. I had my eye on the sweet, crunchy popcorn balls that had become a part of my Spring Fling tradition, along with a new charm for my bracelet, purchased from a friend who crafted charms that were more like works of art than jewelry.

We passed the raffle table where my dentist, Dennis Kramer, was busy selling chances for a shopping spree downtown. "Hey, Dennis, have you seen Eloise?" I asked. In addition to his dental practice, he owned a florist shop next to Olde World Treasures, where Eloise and her sister Greta sold a mix of antiques and old maps with an emphasis on maps. I explained the situation at the plant booth, and he looked up with a frown.

"She seemed fine last night when I went by to close the shop," he said. "With Greta out of town, she wasn't planning on opening the store till late this afternoon— so she could work the booth." Nothing new right there. Greta and Eloise, both getting on in years, operated on a schedule that could be best described as "open by chance or whim."

"Well, I'm checking the store now," I said. "We're thinking she forgot."

Dennis stared down at the ground, not speaking for a moment, and that got *me* worried. Quiet wasn't normal for the big man in the Kramer's Florist T-shirt, who normally had a joke (the world's worst joke, in fact) for any topic that came up.

"I'm sure she's fine," I said. Most likely she was humming some old song as she rearranged some of the items on the shelves, the plant booth having slipped her mind completely. What I worried about in truth was how to make my way past my dentist later with my beloved popcorn ball in hand. I would have to take a winding route behind the food tents and past the fine-arts tables, which would be a pain.

Over the past few months, I'd been plagued with dental problems and been given strict instructions to avoid hard and sticky foods. Which I had done till now. But this was *the Spring Fling*, and it wasn't fair at all, having your dentist stationed right outside the food tents at one of your eagerly anticipated once-a-year events.

With my reluctant dog in tow, I made my way past the booths and displays, and I smiled and held my hand up when we passed people that we knew. And then, out of nowhere, Gatsby lowered his head to the ground and let out the most pitiful-ever whine.

"It's okay!" I told him. "You love the Spring Fling! We'll go find Eloise, and maybe you can see Magellan." Gatsby loved the big orange cat the sisters often brought to work at Olde World Treasures. Whenever I stopped in to shop, Gatsby would lie down close to wherever Magellan might be napping, and the two would snooze together until it was time to go.

Thinking in advance, I made a mental note that Eloise and Greta lived in a large apartment just above the store—which would be convenient if I needed to check in there as well.

Then a quick peek at the sky let me know what was causing the increasingly plaintive whimpers coming from my dog—and it wasn't the missed treats. The clouds had turned very dark. There was no rain in the forecast for the day, but it seemed the weather people had gotten this one wrong—very, very wrong. After we left the map store, I'd have to get Gatsby home to his favorite hidey-holes. For such a big, strong-looking dog, he was terrified of thunder.

Major disappointment, but maybe the bad weather would blow over and I could come back and shop.

Luckily, as a light misting wet my arms, the antique shop was in sight. Two maps and a compass were hand-painted on the glass doors, which were flanked by two huge pots overflowing with pink and white mayflowers; at least *they* would like the rain.

As I often did, I thought about the irony of Eloise surrounding herself with old maps. Eloise was smart—one of the most well-read people in our town. (As the owner of the local bookshop, I could say that for sure.) But the truth of the matter was, Eloise Endicott could not follow any kind of map to save her life. She was, in fact, famous for it! Everyone in town was always pointing Eloise in some direction or another, even though she had lived in Somerset Harbor for nearly forty years. Just the year before, she had gotten lost driving two miles from her home to the Bentley Arboretum, where she'd attended the Flower Extravaganza every spring since 1994.

"But Greta always drives!" she'd explained when she finally made it there, looking rather flustered. Her sister had been sidelined with a migraine for that year's event. North or south, east or west; they were all the same to Eloise, and GPS was more confusing to her than a map. The coterie of nieces and nephews had long given up on bringing their maiden aunts into the world of modern tech.

But while they lacked much knowledge of the modern world, the sisters were filled with fascinating insights into the world of old, as told through the antiques they curated for their shelves. One never knew what kind of treasure you might come across during a quick browse. In addition to ringing up any purchase you might make, the proprietors could weave stories about the setting in which the item was first used, painting a vivid picture for you of a time long gone. It was kind of a combination of a store, a museum, and a history book.

As we crossed the street and moved to the door, Gatsby let out a painful cry, straining on his leash—and something in my stomach dropped. This was something more than his "storm-is-coming" whimper—this one went much deeper. He sensed something very wrong, and I trusted Gatsby's gut, because Gatsby loved his people.

In the few years we'd lived in town, my dog had become everyone's best friend. With his exuberant "atomic tail," as we liked to call it, he celebrated everyone's good news, sometimes feeling even more joy than they did. But he'd been known as well to settle on the floor in a whimpering puddle of despair when someone came into the store—even though they were not yet aware of the diagnosis or bad news on the way.

Just like he could sense the thunder before most of us could, he could sense the pain.

Which is why it was with extreme wariness that I tried the doors to Olde World Treasures. Weirdly, I found the doors unlocked, despite a hand-lettered sign that indicated otherwise. "We will be closed this morning. Hope to 'Spring Fling' with you!" Some lights were on inside—left on all night, I guess, for purposes of security—but the store was mostly dark. So, what exactly was the deal with the unlocked door?

Had Eloise, ever more forgetful now, simply neglected to lock up? That in itself was terrifying, given the price tags on some of the objects in the store. And didn't they have some kind of system with an alarm or something? I should have thought of that before I just came in. I braced myself for the blaring to commence any minute now, sending people running. I'd have some explaining to do, I imagined. But only silence followed.

Absently, I noticed some flyers by the door from the booth to promote activities in town. There were several on the ground: beekeeping, spelunking, the homebrewers' club. Since I could not see Eloise shuffling through a cave, they must belong to someone else, someone who had been in recently and maybe was still there. I didn't think the flyers had just been dropped outside, since one of them was kind of stuck between the door and floor, more inside the store than out.

"Eloise?" I called, but I could hear only silence except for Gatsby's fervent whines. Then he let out a cry that was positively mournful and began to pull me toward the back of the store.

"What is it, boy? What's wrong?" I asked as he tugged me past a display of antique perfume bottles and boxes of old keys, past a line of paintings—toward a pair of sensible but name-brand navy flats. Then a horrendous picture began to emerge as my brain processed what it was I was seeing. The flats, you see, were attached to a pair of legs, and there was blood—a lot of blood. I closed my eyes, feeling faint, and when I opened them again, a shimmer caught my eye. And that is when I saw it: the ornate sword plunged into the center of my dear friend's chest.

CHAPTER TWO

*S*tunned, I couldn't speak, the day of friends and food and fun having suddenly turned ghastly.

"Eloise?" I finally managed to get out in a whisper. But the whiteness of her face, the stillness of her body told me she was gone. Feeling nauseated, I stumbled out onto the sidewalk, where the music and the cheerful crowds felt so very wrong.

Across the street, I caught sight of a familiar rounded figure in a white shirt and khakis, a grape snow cone in his hand. *Andy.* Thank goodness it was Andy. What I needed then was a friend, not some anonymous "whoever" I'd get with 911. Andy was police—or he almost was. He'd retired from the force and moved into the field of private investigations, but the chief still called him in for the more important cases. Because Andy—slow and methodical and often grumpy Andy—knew his stuff.

Finding it difficult to speak, I typed out a text. "I need you now. In front of Olde World Treasures. Andy, hurry please."

I watched as he pulled his phone out of his pocket, read the text, and looked across the street. Registering the horror in my eyes, he came toward me at a run just as the rain began to come down harder and a clap of thunder sounded. Absently, I registered the crowds running for the tents.

Andy was with me in a flash. "*What?*" His eyes were wide. "What's wrong?"

"Eloise! She's dead!" I could barely breathe. "As in, Andy, she's been stabbed! One of those swords she sells…a sword…is stuck in her chest!"

I could not believe it. The swords at Olde World Treasures had always been a source of joy and fascination for adults and kids alike. Kids loved to drag their parents in to see the weapons—many of them ancient—that hung out of reach or were displayed in glass containers. Kids also loved the stories about bloody duels and battles the keepers of the shop would tell with an enthusiasm not befitting their grandmotherly personas.

Handing me his snow cone, Andy had transformed into his official role. "Rue, you wait right there." He nodded toward the awning of the florist shop next door, where I could get out of the rain, which had soaked us through and through. "Either I or someone else will be out to ask some questions." His finger was already poised to call for help. "For now, you keep your distance. Someone still could be inside."

With the snow cone dripping onto my fingers, I did as I was told. My heart felt like it was about to beat out of my chest; the day had turned unreal. Eloise had been one of my gran's dearest friends when I would visit Somerset Harbor as a child, long before I dreamed of moving here myself and taking over the Seabreeze Bookshop for my gran. The maps to me back then had seemed almost magical, brought to life by the stories Eloise and Greta told: tales of pirates and buried treasures, secret doors, and enchanted caves hidden among the colorful lines and illustrations.

Eloise had always been the most playful of the two. She just seemed too vibrant, too *alive* to be…well, not be here anymore.

Soon, police were everywhere, cordoning off the area with yellow crime-scene tape. Festival goers looked on with curiosity and shock from whichever tents or overhangs they had managed to scramble to for shelter. The rain, in the meantime, had intensified and was coming down in sheets. I pulled Gatsby closer to the wall in a futile attempt to protect us from the blowing rain. In my nervousness—and to keep the thing from dripping even more—I licked at Andy's snow cone. Even though there was a trashcan just a few feet away, getting to it would require a dash through the rain, which now was coming down so hard it seemed to be raining sideways.

Then Andy was approaching me, and somehow, he'd managed to acquire a big umbrella. Did cops carry them around for moments such as this? In the movies, tragedy so often coincided with a storm that blew in out of nowhere. And, for all I knew, that might be true in real life as well.

Andy's expression was intent. "I'm gonna put you and Gatsby in a car, to get you out of the rain. We've got some questions for you, and then you can get on home and get yourself dried off." While he spoke to me, two officers moved the crime-scene tape to allow a police car to pull up to the curb. Andy helped me in, and we pulled Gatsby in as well. By now, the frightened dog was trembling at my feet. The young cop at the wheel produced towels for us both.

"Who?" I breathed. "Who could have done a thing

like that to Eloise?" A robbery. It had to be, with all that expensive stuff.

Also in my mind was an unspoken question: why did I always find myself involved in murders that, statistically, should almost never happen in an upscale beachside town? But stumble into them I did—like I was some kind of bad-luck charm in cute low-heeled red pumps.

And every time it happened, I felt *compelled* almost to unmask the monsters behind the brutal crimes, to help the police along—much to the chagrin of Andy. Oh, I was not some deluded detective wannabe who abandoned my duties at the store to chase clues all over town. I just poked around a bit, asked questions here and there. Because the answer was always somewhere, right? The key to everything might be hidden in a memory a customer or friend might have no idea could break the case wide open. On my true-crime shelf and in the thriller section, it happened all the time.

"Our guess is robbery," said Andy, confirming my suspicions. "But we'll need to wait for Greta to determine what might be missing from the store."

"Greta." I took a deep breath. "How will she find out?" Eloise's sister had been visiting a friend in Vermont for the past week or so.

"One nephew's still in town. He's being notified right

now, and he will break the news to Greta and bring her back to Somerset ASAP."

Tears stung in my eyes.

The young redheaded cop held out his hand to me. "My name is Fred, Ms. Collier. I'm very sorry for your loss."

"Fred will be assisting with your statement, Rue," said Andy.

I nodded solemnly. "I talked to Dennis for a second before I came over here to check. And he told me Eloise was planning to stay closed until later in the day. So it did not make sense to me to find the door unlocked."

The two men exchanged glances. "So that points to last night as the likely time of death," said Andy. There was something unsettled in his face—beyond the fact that Eloise was lying, stabbed, inside her beloved shop. "Okay, Rue," he said, "let's start at the top. Tell us first what prompted you to come to the shop."

After Fred pulled out a notebook, I described how Eloise had not shown up to work the booth, and I gave them the details of my time at the shop. Gatsby lay his head on my lap, and soon he was asleep as I told my story.

Andy and Fred exchanged another of those looks.

"What she says is consistent with our victim being

just about to close the shop last night when it all went down," said Fred.

"So she was there all night?" I asked, horrified. I hoped the death, at least, was quick.

Gatsby whimpered in his sleep, and I rubbed his head, more to comfort myself than the dog.

"But something doesn't fit," said Andy with a frown. "Time of death is not official, but it is their best guess she died sometime this morning. And with the amount of blood she lost, the death would have come soon after she was stabbed."

"And if she didn't plan to open until this afternoon... well, I don't get it, Andy. What was she doing there today?" I asked.

Andy cleared his throat. "There are lots of people left to question, so, hopefully, we'll see."

"Hard to imagine that it happened while this big crowd was here," I mused, almost to myself.

"A commotion in the far back of the store *could* have gone unheard," Fred said thoughtfully. "She might not have seen the guy in time to scream."

That painted a mental picture none of us cared to see. We were quiet for a moment.

"Well, lots of work to do," said Andy. "Fred here will drive you home." He watched me carefully. "You gonna be okay?"

I nodded gratefully.

The rain by then had slowed to a drizzle. People had begun to come out from their shelters to confer with one another. A sea of blue lights painted moving pictures in the puddles as I watched the colors, deep in thought. "I guess you saw the flyers," I said, almost as an afterthought. "The ones outside the door?"

"Entered into evidence," said Fred.

"But those things could have been dropped by almost anyone," said Andy. "So many people on the streets today." He gave me a different look, one designed to remind me I was a witness, not a cop.

"But one of them, you see, was wedged beneath the door when I walked into the store. Not in a way that the wind would blow it. But like somebody dropped it, either coming in or out. It was more inside the store than out."

"Well, that's something there," said Andy, a spark of interest in his eyes. "We'll be sure to check for prints."

Very possibly related—although it hardly seemed to fit. Like, some guy would pick up a brochure on making honey on his way to a murder?

Still, I was glad I had told them what I saw. In the mysteries I devoured, the author never put a clue in without it meaning something. But this was the real world, in which things never played out quite as neatly.

Resolutions in real life weren't a simple matter of a few hundred pages left to turn as the story arc played out.

We said a quick goodbye as Andy got out of the car. "You take care, okay?" he told me gently. "Gatsby, you look after her, good boy." He reached to pet the dog, and then he was gone.

The rain intensified again as Fred drove me the short distance to my gran's big house with the wide breezy porch. It had been my own home since my gran, in her retirement, set off to see the world and her friends in far-flung places.

I'd have to tell Gran about her friend, news that would break her heart—but all I could do for now was close my eyes as the sky poured buckets of blinding rain onto the car and road.

CHAPTER THREE

he next morning I slept in since we didn't open at the Seabreeze until noon on Sundays. Nestled on the couch with my coffee, I set aside the murder mystery I'd begun the day before in favor of a light and happy rom-com. I need an escape, not more blood and mayhem. But reading was apparently not in the cards for me. Most days, a book could pull me in, but my mind was too unsettled for me to do anything except take Gatsby on his morning walk and then scroll through the TV channels.

A little later, I stepped into the Seabreeze, where my best friend Elizabeth was already in the back, filing vintage postcards in a box. Antiquities by Elizabeth had become the go-to place for antique photos, letters, scrapbooks, and other intriguing peeks into the past.

Now, she flipped her long hair over her shoulder and moved toward me, a soft look of concern pooling in her eyes. She pulled me into a hug. "Unbelievable," she whispered. "Are you okay?"

We hadn't talked or texted since I'd discovered Eloise, but everyone in town would know by now—both about Eloise and about who had found the body. Because of course they knew all about *a murder* in a town where it was common knowledge whose allergies were acting up and who needed a new knee.

As Gatsby ambled toward his bed in the corner, I sank down in a chair near Elizabeth's display. "Honestly, I am not okay. What I saw was brutal."

Across the room from me, a small gray head popped up from behind a box of books waiting to be shelved. My cat Beasley scampered toward me and jumped into my lap. After that, an even smaller head—this one was white—popped up in the same spot with a questioning "meow." That one would be Ollie, who was soon curled on top of my foot.

Elizabeth took a seat beside me, and we were silent for a moment. After a little while, she asked, "A sword? That's the rumor." She scrunched up her forehead. "One of those *antique swords?* That just sounds too bizarre."

"The rumors are correct," I said. Greta had told me once that collectors loved the things. Swords, apparently, were one of those categories of antiques that appealed to different groups—which dealers loved, of course. Military buffs were big on swords, and they were popular as well with those collectors who specialized in various periods of history.

But no one had set out to *steal* the weapon, since they had left it in the store. Had they stolen other swords? What exactly was the motive?

And how had the killer even *gotten* to the sword? The sisters were mostly good about keeping the dangerous items out of reach. But every once in a while, I would see one lying right out on a counter in reach of anyone. Brought out for a customer, perhaps, or ready to ship out.

Greta had been the guilty party one day when Andy and I dropped in to browse. He loved anything to do with history—French history was his favorite—and I loved antique books. The sword, lying on a table, looked about as long as my arm, ending in a sharp point that meant business. Andy stopped to admire the thing before telling Greta in no uncertain terms to keep the deadly-looking weapon out of reach. "The soldier who carried that old thing might be long gone, Greta, but his weapon still can do the job it was built to do. You've got to put that thing away."

Greta had done as he asked, but with a little giggle, as

if the sword was no more dangerous than the porcelain teapot with dainty yellow roses it was laying next to.

Elizabeth's voice brought me back to the present. "Who on earth do they think did that to our Eloise?" she asked. "Did Andy tell you, Rue?" She took a seat beside me.

"No idea," I answered. "But I hope they catch him soon. Or maybe it's a *her*. Who knows?"

It hit me then the culprit might hit other shops as well, although the Seabreeze didn't have the kind of prices one found at Olde World Treasures and some of the other shops. Plus, I always felt a special kind of safety within my book-lined walls. Book people were a special breed, less likely to sneak an item into their purse or jacket—and especially less likely to do violence in the process. Or so I liked to think. One bought a book, after all, to better understand the world—or to improve oneself. Not typical goals, I'd think, of the criminally inclined.

I got up to make some tea, which we served for free—so that hopefully, our readers would linger for a while, browse around the store some more.

"How did things go at our booth?" I asked, anxious to think of anything but murder. The Seabreeze Bookshop, along with the Easton Ames Memorial Library, had set up a literary scavenger hunt for the month of April. It had been promoted at the Spring Fling with a huge brightly colored map of literary landscapes. The goal was to figure out which book was associated with each point on the map. Inside one copy of each selected book (either at the bookshop or library), players could score a coupon from a local merchant. And these weren't wimpy coupons either. Ice cream for a year! Free stays for a week at several of our luxury inns with water views, where a stay in itself was a vacation.

We made it challenging enough that winners would have to really know the literary world to get to the right books first. Okay, who was I kidding? They had to be best friends with Google. They had to ask Alexa! But they would still, in the end, make their way to a book, so it still served the purpose of promoting reading as a source of enrichment.

It had been my idea, but our head librarian had jumped in with enthusiasm, ideas of her own, and her artistic wizardry. Melanie Lee, in fact, had been the one to draw the amazing landscape, which would make anybody long to know the stories behind the inviting pictures, whose violent waves and soaring castles seemed to spring right off the map.

"It went okay," said Elizabeth, responding to my question. "People seemed excited. But we only had three hours to give out the paper maps and not the six that we had planned." With the rain and the murder, the festival had pretty much shut down after the cops arrived. "Luckily," she said, "we managed to keep our stuff nice and dry—which, I have to tell you, was not an easy feat." She smiled at me ruefully. "Who was expecting a monsoon?"

Both our gazes turned to the oversized piece of canvas on which the map was painted. My favorite part was the right-hand corner with the home from *David Copperfield* that was, in fact, a boat. Its door was open wide to reveal a wooden table set with steaming plates of food and vividly colored mugs.

"You know," I said, realizing something with a start. "I think this idea might have been inspired by Eloise and Greta. Because when I was a kid, I loved to study all the maps they had up in the store. It was my favorite thing."

Their niece Laurel had been my best friend in the summers when I'd visit Gran, and what a time we'd have. Greta was always bringing sweets into the store for all the kids—sweets you would not believe. Laurel had about a zillion cousins who'd all come into town for weeks at a time, as did I. And Eloise would walk around with us throughout the store, telling tales about the maps and what had happened down this little squiggly line or behind this picture of a fortress on a lake. They were not true stories; they were much more fun than truth.

Actually, I think that might have been the place where my love of stories started. Not with books at all—because the fairies, unicorns, and talking elephants all sprung fully formed out of the imagination of Laurel's Aunt Eloise. I took a sip of tea—blueberry-pomegranate—and let my mind go back there for a minute.

"Laurel should be coming in today, I would imagine." I set down my teacup. Along with all of Eloise's family, who were scattered now all across New England. My former friend and I had only kept in sporadic touch since our time as girlhood besties. We'd like each other's posts on Facebook and maybe grab a lunch or a glass of wine every few years or so. "I should run over and check later on if things at the store are slow."

"I wouldn't count on it." Elizabeth's eyes moved to the door, where several customers were already seated outside on the benches, waiting for the store to open. Patiently, they checked their phones and talked quietly amongst themselves.

Elizabeth was right. What was I even thinking? Today we would be slammed. I had learned early on to count on robust business when big news broke in town. On a day like today, people loved to gather and compare notes with one another; everybody wanted to make their opinions known. Somerset Harbor loved to talk, and my gran had wisely made the Seabreeze Bookshop into a place where they could do just that. Thus, the comfy chairs, the free delicious tea, and the stay-and-sip mentality she had carefully curated.

Soon I opened the door for the small waiting crowd, and they just kept on coming in as the afternoon wore on. Gatsby was beside himself with delight when the store was full, and I loved the hum of business and the hope that people would find some joy or comfort in the books they chose. Only Ollie and Beasley were disgruntled over so many "intruders" encroaching on their space at once. But they had lots of little cubbyholes to hide away in and get comfy while they people-watched.

The aisles and seating nooks filled up as people passed around all kinds of "facts" about the murder. Three people claimed to know the exact type of sword that had been used to kill Eloise: a highly collectible piece used by Japanese samurai, a "gentleman's fencing sword" of Italian origin, an infantry officer's sword that dated back to World War One. They had heard it from their aunt or from their friend who was a cop. They had heard it from their barber "in strictest confidence."

Some looked to me for confirmation. But Japanese? Italian? I had no idea. It was long and pointy, which I guessed did not exclude any of the above.

It was after four when things slowed down a bit. Alone in the store, Elizabeth and I scurried to put books back in place, both of us relishing the quiet, which wouldn't last for long. The silence was broken only by a spurt of comments from our parrot Zeke, who could sometimes be a source for intriguing gossip. His cage was in a corner where people thought their whispers would not be overheard. What they didn't know was, parrots have big ears.

Today, however, I was in no mood for gossip as Zeke called out random comments he had overheard.

"Sold me a jade ring that I treasure."

"Italian provenance. Marble! Very fine."

"Watch out for family."

"Greed will get you every time."

"The ones that you keep close are the ones to break your heart."

I glanced at Elizabeth and she glanced back, wide-eyed.

CHAPTER FOUR

The parrot's unexpected words set my thoughts to spinning. I had already planned to seek out Laurel and offer my condolences. But now that little mission might need expediting. A little chat with Laurel and some time spent among the Endicotts could yield up some clues.

I suspected, though, that whatever Zeke had heard was nothing more than gossip. Sure, the close-knit family group was sometimes known to argue—maybe even loudly—but always with a sense of teasing. And always ending up in a round of hugs and laughs. As a child, I'd been a little jealous of Laurel's fun extended family.

Our part-timer Carole was, conveniently, on her way to the bookshop, so now would be the time for me to run out. Andy had said the family would need to let the cops know ASAP if anything was missing. So it was my guess that some of them would be gathered at the store by now to help Greta check the inventory.

Gossip or no gossip, it was important to me to give Laurel a quick hug. Despite the fact we'd grown apart, she and I had been close for several years as we morphed from children to pre-teens. We had comforted each other through a lot of crises—or what seemed like crises in our minds. Eventually, as we grew older, each of us spent less time visiting family in Massachusetts over the summer months. But before then, I'd helped Laurel through her parents' divorce, and she had talked me down after I failed to get a place on the Mustangs Swim Team. I was eleven then, and I thought my life was over. But the carefree, offbeat Laurel had proved to be the perfect friend for a time like that. "Swimming is for fish," she'd said. "It is so much cooler to skateboard really fast." And we had done just that, to the detriment of my skinned knees, but to the freeing of my spirit. We went down hills that summer just like we were flying—with smiley faces and big pink flower stickers plastered on our boards.

Because I was a sheltered, pampered only child, Laurel—who always had that air of being older and just a little dangerous—was someone I had wholeheartedly put my faith in. If it came out of Laurel's mouth, the naïve pre-teen Rue believed that it was true. Now, the memory of some of Laurel's "great ideas" made me wince. But her heart had been pure if her spirit had been wild. She'd gotten me through a lot back then, and now my time had come to be there for her.

I grabbed my purse and told Elizabeth and Carole I would not be gone for long.

"Take your time. We've got this," said Elizabeth.

I gave her a little wave and headed out, glad to escape the voices and the crowd. As I made my way along the downtown streets, the air seemed heavy still with the memory of the rain from the day before. But the sun was peeking out a little from above the canopy of trees that lined the neatly landscaped streets. As I got closer to my destination, I could see a lot of lights on in the store and a sizeable group of people moving around inside.

Someone had left the door cracked open, so I slipped inside and glanced around. It seemed mainly to be the cousins who had gathered—the grown-up "kids" about my age. Was Laurel there? I wasn't sure. She was tall and thin with wispy hair so blonde it was almost white, but then again, so was almost every cousin in the room.

Okay, how sad was this, that so much time had gone by, I had to look real closely to pick out my friend. The one looking through the drawers at the front desk, next to the greasy takeout bags? The one carefully studying a stack of maps? Not Laurel and not Laurel.

But I did see Magellan. The big orange cat was lounging on the counter, rolled onto his back to display his ample tummy.

Then I was distracted by some angry voices to my left. It was two of the guy cousins. One had his hands spread out in disbelief. "Why are you accusing *me*? Man, I didn't take it! I knew you wanted it, that all of us had our eye on putting it up in our houses. And I was gonna wait to see how the will played out. You know, when the time came for that."

"All I know is that it's gone," said the other guy, "and that you're the one who lives here! Who else could get to it so easy?"

Harry Potter's Owl! Were they fighting about *stuff?* When not that long ago, Eloise was lying back there on the floor with a sword through her chest. What was up with these two?

"Will the two of you just shut it?" called a girl from the back. "Someone will overhear, and this is family stuff."

The best response to that—not being a member of the family and all—was to duck behind an antique screen sitting by the door.

"I just find it real suspicious," said one of the girls. Standing in the center of the store, she put her hands on her hips. "I find it real suspicious that the *only thing* that's missing is the map that meant so much to me. I even traveled there my junior year to see it for myself! No one else did that! Newcastle upon Tyne—oh, yeah, I was there. But did I ask to have the map? I didn't. Because I knew it was up to the aunts to decide."

"Hold on just a minute." It was Laurel's voice. "What exactly is it, Krista, you're accusing us of doing?" I could see her and Krista fairly well through the cracks between the panels of the screen.

"I am not accusing anyone of killing her of course!" said her white-blonde lookalike. "I would never think that in a million years. It's just about the map."

"So, the question of the day is, do we tell *the cops* we have a missing map?" The question was posed by a big guy, who seemed to be concentrating more on his lobster roll than any kind of sorting task. "If someone took the thing, they need to fess up now. So the cops aren't searching for some missing map that someone from the family has hidden in a drawer." He paused, and when he spoke again, I could hear his voice start to break. "Because we need the cops to concentrate on who killed Aunt Eloise. Because she was the best."

His plea was met with silence. Magellan wandered

back behind the screen and meowed a hello. *Shoot.* I put a finger to my lips.

Then another girl spoke up—one I couldn't see. "Well, I say we don't tell the cops till we work this out between us. No need to go airing the Endicott family drama all over town."

One of the guys in the front spoke up. "Plus, we don't even know if something else is gone. That's gonna take a while. Because, guys, I have to say it: their record-keeping is as antiquated as some of the stuff they sell."

Okay, I had to get out of there—very quietly. I'd catch up with Laurel later.

I heard her pipe up from the back. "Okay, you guys, this is weird. Come back here, everybody."

As they all rushed to the back, my mind was screaming, *What? What do you see, Laurel?* But this was my chance to scoot out while no one was up front.

I slipped out from behind the screen, tripping over a stone rabbit by the door and knocking down a wooden stool.

"What was that?" a girl asked. "Shoot. Is someone here?"

I heard a rush of footsteps as I darted quickly into the fudge store next door. Thank goodness there always was a crowd for me to blend in with at Something Sweet by Sue. Best peanut butter fudge in the state of Mass-achusetts.

As I stood in line, careful to face away from the door, I pondered what I'd heard. I too had loved the Newcastle map with its bright colors and hand-painted scenes. Of all the maps in the store, it had held the most magic for me—and, it seemed, for the others too. Each time I would visit, Eloise would point to a different spot on the special map and weave a different tale of a secret garden or a long-lost love. My favorite was the castle with the absentminded king who spent his days building paper ships to sail on the River Tyne.

After about a ten-minute wait, I finally placed my order and got some fudge for myself (and for Elizabeth, who was fond of their red-velvet flavor). By that point, enough time had gone by that I felt it was safe to head out the door. Even if I happened to run into Laurel, I would look innocent enough among the crowd, all of us with our small pink boxes that said "Something Sweet by Sue."

Still, I felt unsettled by the argument I had overheard —and by my quick escape that had almost ended badly. Plus, I was still on edge from finding Eloise. It was just the kind of mood that made me glad to have some chocolatey peanut butter to stuff into my mouth. I was savoring my first bite when I almost ran smack-dab into Dennis Kramer, who was ambling around the corner.

"Rue! Hello!" He looked down at my pink box with the little bear that was part of the fudge-shop logo. Fudge was on my no-no list, and here was my frowning dentist. *Huckleberry Finn on the Mississippi*. I was trying desperately to chew, chew, chew so I could quickly swallow. But I had taken a large bite.

Up to then, I had been a model patient. I had only grabbed the fudge at the height of a crisis situation. I had missed my popcorn ball, for goodness sake, and I would not have another chance to get one until the next Spring Fling. And *I had found a body.* For the love of Edgar Allen Poe, give the girl a break—and a peanut butter brownie. Please.

Dennis shook his head at my attempts to hide the sweets. "We're both grownups. My job is to *advise* you, not to scold. It's been a rough time for us all."

Rough enough I didn't even get a signature bad joke. I chewed and chewed, managing at last to swallow all the chocolate. "Hello, Dennis. How are you?"

"I am hanging in there. I finished early with my patients, so now I'm heading over to check in with the florist. As soon as the family announces the arrangements, things at Kramer's will explode. We'll be making wreaths and filling vases as fast as we can get them out. Gotta be prepared."

"Oh yeah, that makes sense." The urge to cry returned. "This whole thing seems unreal."

"Same here. Absolutely. I saw her and Greta nearly every day, but it was Eloise who had the sense of humor." Dennis shook his head. "I had a lot of map jokes saved up for Eloise. We had a lot of laughs."

I gave him a wink. "Eloise was kind. Unlike those of us in your chair, *she* could have told you that your jokes aren't remotely funny. Most of us never get the chance, you know. With our mouths all filled with tools."

He gave a little chuckle. He did not throw back his head and laugh like he might have done any other week, but he laughed all the same. "Now you know my secret. Captive audience!" He reached around to pat my back. "You take care now, Rue."

And then off we went, Dennis to his flowers and me to my books, both of our hearts a whole lot heavier than the week before.

The only question was, why was Dennis heading *away* from the florist? Was he keeping secrets too?

CHAPTER FIVE

*T*hat night I texted Andy to come over for a drink. When his work was extra busy, he didn't come around that much. His cases kept him frantic—but he had other reasons too. He was always saying that I was too nosy about "official business" and "confidential" stuff that was only for the cops to know.

Nosy—what an ugly word. How much nicer it would be to say I was *concerned* about the place in which I made my home. And this time, I was sick to the point of being nauseated over Eloise.

"Gatsby cordially invites you to the porch for a glass of whiskey." I sank down on the couch and typed in the message after I'd kicked off my shoes and let down my hair.

Andy loved his whiskey, but more than that, he loved my dog. His private-investigation work kept him super stressed even when he wasn't being pulled in by the cops to help them with a case. And he always said my gran's front porch had the essential elements of comfort: a good dog, a fine glass of whiskey, a breeze that smelled of sea, and a friend in the rocking chair next to him. Both of us lived alone and liked a little company to help us wind down the day.

His answer came back quickly. "Does 7:15 work? I can bring us sandwiches from Melba's. Special of the day: shrimp po'boys and two sides."

Now, that was a plan I liked. I was always telling Melba she should bottle up the remoulade she put on her to-die-for po'boys. The tourists would eat it up.

I sent Andy a thumbs-up then changed into my most comfortable sweats and tee. Then, with a glass of pinot blanc and a book in hand, I sat down on the porch swing and shut my eyes for a moment. It felt nice to just take in the quiet, two cats on my lap and one dog at my feet. It had been a week.

Seeing Andy would be good to get me out of my funk, and I'd see tomorrow if Melanie was free for lunch. More times than not the two of us would get so tickled over something we'd be reduced to tears. And that was the feeling I was craving hard; I needed to forget, even if it only lasted through the course of a Cobb salad and a coffee.

The two of us had grown closer over the last few weeks as we put our heads together for the treasure hunt. But Melanie had been a friend since I moved to town. Some of my customers liked to tease me about being friendly with the "competition." As the head librarian in town, Melanie pretty much lent out for free the things I was selling. But we had always worked together to promote the joy of reading. And that created more book buyers in the town—and more book borrowers as well, depending on the readers' budgets.

In addition to our project with the literary treasure hunt, we ran a book club as a team. (Melanie had several of them going.) Plus, she and I would sometimes pick a book to read together and discuss. Her fun takes on the classics had been known to make me laugh so hard I snorted, which more than once had earned me dirty looks in the Easton Ames Memorial Library, where silence was a virtue. Only Melanie would use *The Bachelor,* of all things, to talk about classic lit. "Edward Rochester, in the back row with your piercing eyes, will you accept this rose?"

Not that my snarky friend couldn't in her turn be

serious and deep. Like no one else I'd ever known, she could zero in on the heart of any story and make a book say something huge about my life or hers. Or the lives of the Tuesday Evening Readers, the club we ran together. To talk books with Melanie was to talk about the parts of life that mattered most—and her wisdom could clarify and comfort and affirm.

I sent her a text. "Lunch tomorrow. Noon? At the Oregano and Olive? We need to pick a theme for next year's book club soon." A new year started for the club at the end of every August. I'd found that when school began, a lot of grown-ups in the town craved that sense of a fresh start for themselves as well—and the smell of brand-new books.

I read and dozed a little until Gatsby startled me with his enthusiastic greeting of his best friend, Andy. I looked up and smiled as Andy ambled up the walk, a plastic bag in hand.

"Gatsby! Calm down, please." I couldn't help but laugh as my dog almost knocked Andy over, his "atomic tail" a blur.

Andy knelt down on the sidewalk to rub the big dog's ears. "This is one of the many gifts that dogs bring into our lives. They mistake a boring bachelor with a bad knee for some kind of king. And that feels awfully good." He got up from the sidewalk and walked up onto the porch, setting down the takeout bag on a wicker table.

"You look exhausted, Andy." I worried for him often. And I could see the line between his brows was extra deep today.

He settled at the table. "Well, we're all going at it hard, as you can imagine." He looked out at the trees. "It's nice to rest my mind."

I poured some whiskey for him and another glass of wine for myself. Then we ate and drank in a companionable silence as scenes from the nightmare week ran through my head. Andy, I could tell, had stuff to process too. I often wondered how he could hear so many details about humans at their worst and not let it get to him more.

I took a bite of sandwich. The shrimp were flavorful and crispy, and the remoulade, of course, was the best thing in the world.

"Progress on the case?" I asked. I had some ideas for a few things they could do to that sword-wielding miscreant. I would absolutely love to have a go at him myself with something really sharp.

"Well, we did get some prints off the weapon, which is a major deal." Andy took a sip of whiskey, then he sighed. "But this case is an odd one. Because here's what I don't get: The perp *should* have been all bloody—highly visible, you see. And it's almost like he *had* to have left through the front door—and on the morning of the Fling. When people would have noticed a bloody, fleeing man." He frowned thoughtfully.

"What makes you think he didn't slip out through the back?" Behind Olde World Treasures was a small parking lot, only used by staff. Behind that was just a vacant wooded lot.

"You said the front door was unlocked when you went in that day. And the only other door—the one in back—was locked up tight. The medical examiner is fairly certain she was stabbed the morning of the Fling. And the committee and the vendors were on site before the sun went up. Setting up the booths, preparing all the foods. A man in bloody clothes would have been awfully hard to miss."

I took a sip of wine. "I get what you're saying. That is odd."

Andy *must* be tired, I thought. This was what he normally would refer to as "confidential business"—or, in other words, off-limits to the likes of me.

"Could he have somehow found a key?" I asked. "And locked the back door when he left?" Although that seemed odd as well: a crook who took a life then remembered to lock up.

Andy shook his head. "We don't believe he had a key. Because this doesn't read to us like a well-planned crime. This was not a guy who came prepared to kill; he used a weapon, for example, that he found on the scene, not one he brought himself. So it's doubtful that the guy planned out his escape route enough to procure a key before he did the deed."

"Unless there was just a key laying out for him to find," I said. If the elderly sisters could get a little careless about leaving *swords* around, they might do the same with keys.

"But Eloise's key was in her purse, which we found on the scene. And Greta still has hers."

"*Greta.* How is Greta?" Tears pricked at my eyes.

Andy shook his head. "Like she lost her other half. Which I guess she has."

"So not a robbery, I guess—if he left the purse right there."

"Oh, robbery is still our best theory for a motive." Andy took a bite of his sandwich. "Lots of pricey stuff to take, but not much in the purse. A comb, four dollars and some change, and fifty wads of tissue."

Gatsby trotted over to his friend and looked eagerly at Andy, who gave him a fry.

I bit into my sandwich and felt a sharp pain in the back-right portion of my mouth. "Bartholomew Cubbins's hats—that hurts!"

"You okay?" asked Andy.

"It's just this trouble with my teeth." I winced. This time it was really bad. If I could have *just remembered* to chew on my left side, it would have been okay. But in my delight over the po'boy, I forgot. All I could do was close my eyes and wait for the pain to go away. Like I needed *this* with all the other stuff I was dealing with this week.

I settled back against the seat and told myself I'd be okay. I'd be seeing Dennis soon, and he had promised to fix me up as good as new. Even if that "fixing up" might leave me without my wisdom teeth. That was a procedure I'd been putting off for years.

"We'll have you chewing like a champ," Dennis had told me with a smile on my last visit. "Majorly important in this land of plenty, home of the world's finest lobster rolls and jumbo scallops."

To get my mind off the pain, I threw another question at the very chatty Andy—before he suddenly remembered he didn't like to chat with me about a case. "Please tell me that you have a suspect. Or that you have a lead at least. Because it creeps me out to think I could be *walking down the sidewalk* tomorrow with a monster—

or selling him a book. What if the guy comes in my store?"

Plus, this was a crime that couldn't go unpunished.

Andy's answer was a sigh. "I wish I could tell you something different—that we have some likely suspects. But it could have been a random crime of opportunity. By some out-of-towner, long gone from here by now. And if she was targeted...well, there's not a lot to go on there. Eloise was not a woman with a list of enemies. Hardly anybody ever spoke a harsh word to—or about—Eloise." He took a sip of whiskey.

"*Hardly* anyone?"

He looked me in the eye, considering how much to tell me. "This is between you and me?"

"Of course."

He let out a sigh. "This can go no further than this porch. I know I'm running my fool mouth much more than I should. But, Rue, I need to vent."

I reached out to touch his hand. "You're in your safe space, Andy. What is spoken on the front porch *remains* on the front porch. Or however that old saying goes."

Ollie leaped up in his lap as if to reassure him.

"And that goes for the pets," I added. "Ollie here's a master secret-keeper."

Andy rubbed along the cat's soft back. "The older that I get, it seems, the more things get to me. And this case is a hard one; I've known Eloise forever—her and Greta too. I used to cut their lawn back when I was a kid. And they'd give me silver dollars for my birthday and when I graduated and sometimes just because."

With no children of their own, Eloise and Greta had "adopted" a string of local kids. Children were welcomed with enthusiasm in the shop, despite the pricey, often fragile merchandise that lined the shelves. A jar of suckers always sat at the front counter in flavors that enticed: grape and lime and cherry, making for a memory that I could almost taste. A basket of inexpensive "antique" toys was set out for kids to touch, and touch we always did during the childhood summers I spent in Somerset Harbor with my gran.

"And some of the calls that have come into the station..." Andy continued to describe the difficult nature of the case. "We have to follow up on every lead, of course, but some of them seem absurd." He stared into his glass, which by now was empty. "Or that might just be my bias. Because I don't want to think it was one of us—part of my little 'family' here in Somerset. Maybe even someone that I liked."

"It would be really tough to find out a thing like that," I said, being very careful not to jump in with a "Who?" He'd answer in his own time when—and if—he chose. There was something on his mind, and I would bide my time. Plus, tonight he was in need of someone who'd just listen.

I pushed aside my plate with the other sandwich half, which would be tomorrow's dinner. And we sat in silence for a moment as the white pines danced a little in the breeze.

"The weapon," Andy said, "was French. A rapier sword that once belonged to a Napoleonic officer—a dream find for a collector. It had a gold gilt hilt, Rue. The details were just stunning. I don't know how much you might remember from that day." He ran a hand over his head. "I would have told you on another day that it was a thing of beauty." He stared down at the floor. "If it had not been used to kill and torture a seventy-six-year-old very fragile lady, as sweet as they come."

Andy was a history buff and spent a lot of time in that section of my store when his workload allowed. French history, especially, seemed to fascinate him.

"Sounds expensive," I said. "Do you think a sword like that was what the killer wanted? And then he just freaked out and left it there when things went wrong?"

"Could be. Or he might have been conducting a more extensive theft. We still don't know from the family if any items from the store have turned up missing."

Well, there was that missing map. But that seemed more sentimental than of monetary value—compared to the Chinese vases, German porcelain, and rare clocks priced in the thousands. The business with the map seemed more like family drama than any kind of clue. I'd let Andy know, of course. But I'd have more information—hopefully—when I caught up with Laurel. And I planned to do that soon.

The wind picked up, blowing harder through the trees as the moon shone down on the pines. I picked up my glass of wine.

"Melanie Lee," said Andy.

My heart seemed to freeze. "What about her, Andy?"

"She's the one I mentioned—that we've had calls about."

I almost spit out my drink. "But, Andy, that's just crazy. Are you even serious?"

"Two people reported arguments between her and Eloise. It happened in the store—in the past week or so." He paused. "More than arguments, I'd say. It got rather heated, Rue. Or Melanie was heated. Eloise, we understand, stayed calm. But was visibly distraught."

I could barely speak. I had never seen Melanie lose her temper even once. "But I don't... Why in the world... Arguments *about what?*" What he was saying seemed unreal.

"No one seemed to know the source of the disagreement." He looked me in the eye. "But threats were overheard. On more than one occasion." His eyes went to the floor. "I'm really sorry, Rue. I know the two of you are friends. And chances are that none of this is related to the death."

Because of course it couldn't be. I breathed in and out. Angry words were one thing, and murder was another.

My phone buzzed on the table. Crazily, it was Melanie responding to my text just minutes after Andy had brought her name into the conversation. I looked down to see a long gray mass of words, which was typical of her. We were "word people" after all. My bookish friend was known to send long, rambling texts, kind of stream of consciousness, and this was no exception.

"Lunch sounds great. Let's do it," she had written. "And about the book club, I was thinking we could do a theme involving…murder. I've seen a lot of newer books with the same kinds of story lines: decent, caring people who find themselves caught up in extraordinary circumstances. Books that explore the question: why do people who are basically honorable human beings find themselves doing things they never dreamed they'd do? Lately I've been drawn to those kinds of plots. But is that too much, considering the news?"

She had been *drawn* to those? My heart rate was off the charts.

Some people turned to books as a source of escape. But I knew that others found a comfort in seeing their own lives mirrored on the pages.

Andy's words broke into my thoughts. "I know the two of you hang out. Have you noticed anything that's off?"

"Well, she hasn't seemed upset or mad. She's kind of loose and easy. Goes with the flow, you know? And she's never mentioned Eloise in all the time I've known her. And surely she would never…"

"Oh, I know, I know."

I don't think even Andy knew how close I'd become to Melanie over the past few weeks. The planning for our "literary trail" had inspired some discussions that went on late into the night. And we'd found we had a lot in common: historical fiction with medieval settings, literary fiction with surprising twists, police procedurals, and Mario Kart on the Nintendo.

Then I made my mind up to do what I had to do. "I haven't noticed anything that's off, but I just got this." I slid my phone to Andy, feeling like a traitor. I felt like I was being tested—like one of those "decent" protagonists in "extraordinary circumstances." I hoped I'd passed the test.

Andy read and frowned. "Interesting," he said.

I took a sip of wine. "Please solve this one, Andy. It's messing with my head."

Finding Eloise had been horrific, and I couldn't help but wonder if the solving of the thing would break my heart again.

CHAPTER SIX

 he parking lot at the Easton Ames Memorial Library was filled with minivans and SUVs, not unusual for a late weekday morning. Mom and Tot Story Hour; or, as Melanie liked to call it, rush hour in the stacks.

I opened the glass doors and headed to my right. The plan was to browse the staff picks while I waited for my lunch date to finish with her story and the related craft. Thankfully, I'd managed to sleep well and ease my mind somewhat after hearing Andy's news. Melanie was *Melanie*, who'd just had a little tiff with a local merchant —who happened to be murdered not long after that. People argued all the time, and those disagreements hardly ever ended with people getting killed.

I was, nonetheless, still a little jumpy from the week's

events—and anxious to find the special sense of peace that seemed to be unique to the libraries of the world. I was breathing in the scent of books when I felt a sudden jolt, someone pushing hard into my chest.

With a little scream, I jumped back, and I almost lost my breath when I looked down to see...was I looking at *a sword?*

I was.

It seemed to have been fashioned out of tinfoil and cardboard with fake jewels down the side. The thing was being brandished by a child with furry bear-like ears and a nose that had been painted brown.

I let out a deep breath. It was a toy, just a toy. A rather startling toy, given what the town was going through, but still...

"Who goes there? Bonjour!" The boy spoke in a high-pitched voice and watched me with narrowed eyes. "Have you come to explode the world or have you come to save it?" asked the child.

"I come in peace, so carry on. Save our planet. Please!"

He watched me, unsure. "You don't *look like* a llama."

"Okay! Well then...thanks?" I *guessed* it was a compliment—of sorts, anyway.

The room had grown much louder, which led me to believe the class had just let out. The aisles were filled with "bears" with tinfoil swords gleaming in the light. The bear next to me began to spin in circles.

A young mom with a ponytail rushed up to take my new friend by the hand. "Peter Michael Clarkson, would you stop spinning, please? You'll get so dizzy you'll be sick." Then she caught my eye. "Forgive us, please. I'm sorry! My son just gets...excited. And he loves Pierre the Bear—who saved the world from flying kumquats manned by evil llamas." She paused thoughtfully. "A cute book and all of that. But after..." She glanced down at the boy and lowered her voice to a whisper. "After, well, *you know*...was it such a good idea to have the kids make *swords?* The timing just seems bad."

Parents were doing their best to separate young dueling bears before things got out of hand. And in the middle of it all was my tall, dark-haired friend, holding up her own sword while the children clapped and laughed.

"I guess there wasn't time to change the book?" I said to the mom.

Except who was I kidding? The shelves were over-flowing in the children's section. So many, many books.

Then Melanie caught my eye and waved, a big grin on her face. Soon she was beside me, pulling off her furry ears. "Hey! I am *so* ready for some pesto tortellini. These kids wear me out."

A small bear hugged her knees, and Melanie bent down to hug the bear goodbye. "It was fun," she told her. "Find you some good books to take home."

"You want to walk?" I asked her. "I've got so much nervous energy. I need some exercise."

The Oregano and Olive was just two blocks away, and so off we went, taking in the sea breeze as we walked.

"Kind of crazy, really, that you would choose that book," I said. "Considering…you know."

Melanie brushed her wispy bangs out of her face. "Yeah, I do get what you're saying. Do you think it was too much?"

"Oh, I don't know. It's fine. It's just a children's story. I'm still just shaken up, I guess."

"Rue, I'm sorry. I heard you were the one who… That must have been just… Well, I can't *imagine* how you must have felt."

We walked along in silence, and I waved to Reg from the men's shop, who was darting into the dry cleaner's.

"I should have thought it out better than I did." Melanie adjusted the strap of the small pink purse she wore over her shoulder. "I've just always loved that book. And did I ever tell you that my dad collected swords? His specialties were antique Asian swords, pirate replicas, and collectors' versions of famous movie swords." She paused. "But I can also see that now was not the time."

Since I really needed to get my mind off the murder, I quickly changed the subject. We talked books and to-be-read lists, and we continued that discussion at the restaurant while we enjoyed our food. My friend also filled me in on the latest meeting of her classics book club. It was called What the Dickens? and had met the night before. She ran a lot of book groups, but I'd always felt she took a special pleasure in this one. She made it a kind of mission to introduce local readers to the great books of the world she thought everyone should read.

"Thanks for coming out with me," I said as I took a bite of the chocolate-chip cannoli dish we'd ordered for dessert. "I knew you were the one to get me out of my head."

She reached out to grab my hand. "You sure you're okay?"

I shook my head. "I just can't seem to get that picture of Eloise out of my head."

Her eyes filled with sympathy, and she squeezed my hand. "It was hideous what happened, no two ways about it. But here's what you should do—or you should *try to*, anyway. Replace that picture in your mind with the thought of Eloise when she was alive. Like, with a cup of tea and telling some long story about one of her antiques." Then Melanie grew quiet, lost in thought. "She always lived her life with a kind of childlike joy, you know? One moment of horror, Rue—but so much, *so much* joy."

I watched her carefully. "Had you seen her lately?"

She answered with a shrug. "I don't go in there all that much. With a county salary, I'm not one to shop for vintage rugs from Morocco or wherever."

"I used to imagine some of those creations spread out in my foyer. Some of those things are exquisite." I reached for my latte. "So. You haven't been there in a while?"

Melanie shifted, uncomfortable, in her seat. "I was not a regular. But I've been known to browse."

"When was the last time you were in?"

She reached for her purse. "Just let me check my messages real quick. The board of directors has a meeting in the morning, and they keep texting endless questions."

Obviously, her last talk with Eloise was not up for discussion.

I took a sip of latte. "I can't believe she's gone. That I can't just pop in after lunch and browse the maps while she tells me about her garden or some silly something that she read in her gossip magazines."

Melanie picked up her coffee mug. "Well, those days

were about to be over anyway. Which is just so weird after all these years." She took a sip of coffee. "Yeah, even if Eloise had lived, we would have lost the store."

I paused, a spoonful of cannoli halfway to my mouth.

She noticed my expression. "Oh! You hadn't heard? They were gonna sell, you know."

"I had no idea!"

"Oh, yeah. Brenda from Beckham Properties is in my classics book club, so I know all about it. And she told me Greta came into the office about two weeks ago. She was asking Brenda how much they might expect if they put their building up for sale." She gave me a knowing look. "Greta, from what I understand, was *intent* on selling."

"But it's always been a map shop!" I could not imagine Franklin Street without it—a bit of my childhood magic gone. Of course, I knew both owners were getting on in years, and the younger family members were scattered over several states. None of them seemed much inclined to sell antiques. Still, both the sisters had always seemed to think of the place as "home." I had just assumed they would keep it going as long as they could.

In fact, earlier this month, Eloise had joked about working in the store until she turned a hundred. "Who wants to retire?" she'd asked, waving the thought away. "I can sit upstairs, all alone with Greta, or I can come down here to my happy place with my maps and all the shoppers who come by to say hi. As long as my health holds, I'll choose option B."

Which made sense to me. If the sisters chose to sleep in, if they were feeling tired, or if something good was on TV, they just stayed closed for the morning—or the day, whatever suited them. If they felt like company, they opened up the store. A nice life if you could get it.

"What you're telling me is crazy." I sat back in my chair. "Because I'm almost sure that Eloise planned to keep her life exactly as it was."

"Yeah, it did seem weird to me. But Brenda swore that Greta had her mind made up; she was gonna sell." That was followed by a pause. "Oh, Rue, do you know what? Brenda might have meant for me to keep that to myself. Because, well, I don't know...is that stuff supposed to be, you know, *confidential*, between a client and an agent? She might not have even told me, except we had a little something planned for What the Dickens? And the store came up as part of the discussion. So, Rue, please zip your lip about that little tidbit." Melanie rolled her eyes. "Me and my big mouth."

"But I don't understand. Did they need the money?" Surely not. The elder Endicotts were fond of the finer things in life and didn't hesitate to show it, wearing Givenchy scarves and eye-popping diamond rings. With most of the charity events I'd been involved with, the sisters had written checks that were beyond generous.

Then I became aware of Melanie eyeing me intently. "Earth to Rue! Where did you go?"

"Oh, sorry! It's just that I'm almost sure that Eloise had no idea about...well, about her sister's little talk with Beckham Properties. Which is kind of weird."

"I just assumed they both agreed. Maybe Greta hoped that Brenda would throw out some big number to change her sister's mind."

"Maybe? I don't know." Something just felt wrong.

I bit into my bite of cannoli then, and something else felt wrong—on the inside of my mouth. "Whoa." My hand flew up to my cheek. I thought the sharp pain in my gum would slice my mouth wide open. Stupid, stupid me. Why could I not remember to chew *on the left?* This pain was way worse than before.

"You okay?" My friend looked alarmed.

"My stupid teeth again." Hopefully, Dennis had an opening right now—or some good pain meds or something.

CHAPTER SEVEN

"Done in by dessert," I told Dennis with an eye roll. "It tasted sweet, at least, until it almost killed me. It was a chocolate chip, I think." He had fixed me up enough that I could joke about it now. Pain meds were my friend.

My dentist didn't look amused. "It was infected, Rue, which means those wisdom teeth come out. They come out ASAP. I don't think you have a choice."

I guessed he was right. Any bite these days could turn into excruciating pain, and who had time for that?

He steadied himself against the counter, and his face looked ashen.

"You okay?" I asked. "It should be me who's turning white."

He shook his head. "I'm just feeling off today." He

pulled off his gloves. "You hearing any news about the investigation?"

"I wish I could tell you that I heard they caught the monster, but the answer, I'm afraid, is no. Oh, and by the way, did Eloise and Greta have plans to sell the shop?" With my gums all numbed, I slurred my words like I was drunk. I'd have to let Elizabeth deal with customers today while I worked in the back.

And then I remembered I was supposed to zip my lip. Never tell someone a secret right before they take pain meds—really strong pain meds.

Dennis looked surprised. "Oh, my goodness, no." He paused. "Well, Greta, I believe, has been ready for a while to hang it up. She wants to do some traveling—like your gran. But I assumed they'd keep the shop as long as their health allowed. Because of Eloise. She was like a kid on a playground surrounded by her 'toys' when she was in the shop."

That sounded about right. Eloise had still been very much the "baby sister" of the pair. Greta would supervise her sister's starch intake, for example, and place sticky-note reminders on the counter: reminding Eloise to take her pills or pay the water bill. Not that both the sisters didn't have a sense of fun. I could sometimes hear them laughing when I passed the store. It was a musical, happy sound that reminded me a little of a waterfall.

They'd had the same lilt in their voices, the exact same laugh, and the same way of holding their hands over their mouths and crinkling their eyes when they were delighted by a story from a customer or by a new antique that came in.

"Why do you ask?" he said.

"I've just had them on my mind and…wondered."

"I'll bet that place would bring a fortune. Because their store is huge, compared to the florist shop and the other buildings on the block. And I sometimes wondered if it was a source of tension between the two of them, the question of retiring. The last time I was in, they both seemed a little miffed with one another. But sisters will be sisters, right? Even in their seventies."

But the Endicotts were famous for how they got along; Greta had devised a system the two of them had used for decades. On Tuesdays and Thursdays, Eloise would pick where they went for lunch. On Mondays and Wednesdays: Greta's turn. On the other days, they'd bring leftovers from the house. And every other week-end, each sister got to choose an activity or movie. I'd heard there was a schedule even for the remote control. A little much, I thought, but, hey, whatever worked.

Dennis handed me a slip to take to the front so I could pay and make my follow-up appointment to talk about my wisdom teeth.

As I made my way to the desk, I noticed how the office just seemed...different. It was very, very quiet. Normally, Dennis's big voice would follow me as I walked down the hall, and he'd missed a lot of chances for awful jokes today: my chocolate-chip injury, the upcoming loss of my "wisdom" teeth. The staff seemed subdued as well; this place normally lived up to its reputation as the "friendliest dental office in Mass-achusetts."

I got that Dennis was upset about Eloise, who'd had a store next to his florist's shop for more than a decade now. But I also knew that Dennis had a habit of joking his way through hard times. Like the traffic accident that left him with a broken leg last year, and the divorce that at times had been bitter. Joking had always been his way to comfort both himself and others—but today, something just seemed off.

My hygienist, Kara, and Ethel, the receptionist, had their backs to me as I approached the desk.

"...should have just stayed home. The way his hands were shaking!" Ethel was saying in a whisper.

"It's like he's seen a ghost," said Kara. "I've never seen Dennis act like this. Something's up for sure."

"I hope it's not more staff cuts."

"Surely not so soon."

Then they noticed me.

"Rue!" Kara's voice turned cheerful. "I'm starting to think that you're a member of the staff."

"Well, the wisdom teeth are coming out, so maybe that will solve my problems. And then you guys are gonna miss me and my Discover Card," I joked.

I handed my sheet to Ethel, who made an appointment for me in a week and took my card.

"What are these?" I asked, noticing a scattering of toys on the far side of the counter. "Are those the treats for little boys and girls who brush and floss? Is there an age limit for those things, or do I get a treat??"

Ethel laughed. "Oh, those belong to Dr. Dennis. He's had a lot of nervous energy these past two months or so." She rolled her eyes, and Kara shook her head.

"So Ethel got him these," said Kara.

"I thought if he had some little toys to fiddle with, he wouldn't drive us nuts with the knuckle-popping and the rapping on the desk." Ethel leaned in to whisper to me. "It's worse than the bad jokes."

I now recognized that several of the toys were those fidget-spinner things that used to be popular. And there were a couple of squishy balls in lime green and orange. I'd heard them called "stress balls," so it made a kind of sense.

"Whatever gets you through." I gave them a sympathetic smile. "I'll see you both next week."

Back at the store, Elizabeth took care of customers while I holed up in back and did paperwork. Well, mostly I jotted notes in the leather notebook I used for journaling. I was like my dentist—off my game and distracted. So much weirdness in the town since I found the body! Was some of it related? Or just coincidence?

I tried to make a list of facts. One of the nephews or nieces might have taken a map from Olde World Treasures—a map the younger Endicotts seemed to be strangely drawn to. A sentimental choice for some, but weren't there lots of maps that held the magic of the stories their Aunt Eloise and Aunt Greta used to weave?

Did the family know that Greta had plans to sell the store? And how could she sell the store when her co-owner Eloise had been determined they were staying put?

Next, I wrote down "Dennis." Something there was way off too. He'd been in such a mood today. His dental practice seemed to be in trouble, and he'd lied to me in town. He'd told me he was heading to his florist's shop, but then he had very clearly walked the other way.

And there was Melanie, my dear friend, who seemed to have swords and murder on her mind—and who had argued with Eloise not long before she died.

Even the skies above the grieving town seemed to be out of sorts. Much like on the day Eloise was killed, a hard rain had been falling since I got back from my appointment.

I rubbed at my forehead, feeling a headache coming on. Sometimes, putting words to paper helped me clear my mind, but today the list just had me more confused. I wanted to just sleep, like Beasley and Oliver, who were curled up together in a ball in the corner of my office.

The numbness in my mouth was starting to wear off, and my gums began to ache just as a sharp pain pierce my forehead. A headache *and* a toothache? Now, that just wasn't fair.

Which was why the gentle rapping at the door came as a nice distraction. It was Elizabeth with a china cup, and I could smell the comforting aroma of good tea.

"Is it okay now for you to drink a little something?" asked Elizabeth.

"Oh, thank you. Yes, I think so. The numbness is almost gone."

She set the cup and saucer at the edge of my desk and took a seat, keeping the door open in case a customer came in. "The tea is warm but not too hot," she said.

"Thanks. How are things in front?"

"It's been slow with all this rain. This is a day to go

out only if you have to, and 'book emergencies' are rare. How are you doing, Rue? You don't look okay."

I took a grateful sip of the vanilla pomegranate tea. "My thoughts are still wrapped up with Eloise," I said. "I'm trying not to play detective, but I just want to know who—and why. And things in town are weird. Like, I saw Melanie at lunch, and…well, did she seem okay to you when you worked the booth that day?"

The morning Eloise was murdered. Melanie could not have stabbed someone to death and then just waltzed over to a booth at a festival and talked about books and maps. *That* should stop the crazy thoughts going through my head.

"You know, she really didn't seem okay," said Elizabeth. "Even before we knew…you know, what had happened." She pulled her long hair over her shoulder. "Maybe she's just busy. She always does too much. And she had *another* project she was working on, if you can believe it. Trying to pull together some antiques to display in the next few weeks—for her classics book club. This year they're doing Dickens, so she was looking for some stuff from England and the nineteenth century to sit out on the shelves. Which I thought would look really classy. And I got the sense the classics club could use some help bringing in new members." She stretched out her legs. "Maybe *Bleak House* doesn't hold up in the age of the Real Housewives and all that foolishness. We've all become too shallow."

"Oh, Dickens has its share of romantic troubles, family conflicts—all of that. Reality TV doesn't have the edge on over-the-top drama."

"I told her I would help, see what I could find in the way of postcards and letters and the like. Most of what I sell is local, but I have some contacts who deal in stuff from across the pond."

"That does sound very nice."

"Although, I have to say, I was not inclined to help at first. After she showed up so late. It was no fun, let me tell you, working by myself, and there was quite a crowd."

My heart seized up at her words. "Melanie was late?"

"By at least thirty minutes. Very unlike her. And it was busy at the booth."

"Why was she late? Did she say?"

"No, but something had upset her. I could tell. She seemed almost angry. Not like Melanie at all."

I reached for my tea and tried to take steady breaths. There had to be an explanation.

Sip slowly. Breathe in, then breathe out.

It would be okay.

CHAPTER EIGHT

he next day I put up a sign that said the Seabreeze would be closed from twelve thirty to two thirty. It was important to me—and to Elizabeth—to be at First Methodist of the Redeemer for our dear friend's funeral. Our part-timer Carole wanted to be there as well, since Eloise and Greta had teamed up as the leaders of her scout troop way back in the nineties.

Across the street from my shop, Kate Rochelle at Sophisticated Cuts gave me a little wave as she taped her own sign to her door. Except for shops that catered heavily to tourists, things in Somerset Harbor always came to a respectful pause when it was time to say goodbye to one of our own. Deaths seemed to be mourned more deeply among our close-knit group, and births were greeted with more awe. Our fellow merchants felt like family, and it felt personal to us when life began or ended along the well-kept sidewalks of our sun-kissed paradise.

Andy was waiting for me on the bench outside, frowning as he mumbled to someone on the phone. Life never seemed to let poor Andy completely take a pause.

I caught just a few words here and there: "bloody shirt" and "lab." And I thought I heard him say "Barney Stuckey." But that could not be right.

"Further questioning," said Andy. "A few more things to ask."

He was speaking quietly, but I had always had a good sense of hearing, and I could read lips as well. Possibly because even as a child, I'd felt the need to know as much as I could about the other lives going on around me.

I brushed some lint off my black pencil skirt and fixed the strap on my low heels. *Barney Stuckey? Really?* There was no way the eighty-six-year-old frail-as-a-toothpick *Barney* could have stabbed Eloise to death. Maybe Andy had been saying "Arnie Lucky" from the shoe store. Arnie Lucky also did not seem like a felon— but he at least could have picked that sword up without his back giving out.

Barney, though, was the least likely guy in town to be

our killer. Since retiring as a pest-control technician, he'd made deliveries for the florist shop in the blue Ford Maverick pickup he drove around and polished like it was some prize. Barney, plagued by a bad back and emphysema, could barely manage the heavy doors at the antique shop, let alone pick up that sword and...do that to Eloise.

I took a deep breath, trying to erase the picture from my mind of Eloise sprawled on the floor.

Plus, Barney was a giver, not a stabber. If a family was in need, Barney had been known to make an extra stop to pick up a little something extra to go with the delivery. So, the customer would get a cup of coffee or a children's toy or slice of key lime pie to go with their plant or bouquet, compliments of Barney.

Oh, well. Whatever might be going on with Barney (or Arnie) and the bloody shirt (good grief), I would not be getting any answer out of my detective friend—off-limits information. I gave him a smile. "Thanks for coming by."

He answered with a nod.

In fact, I guessed it should be me passing on some information. My best guess was the cops already knew Melanie had been late—and out of sorts—when she showed up to work the booth on the horrendous day

Eloise was found. But I should say something just in case.

I cleared my throat, feeling disloyal to my friend, kind of like that one kid in second grade I used to despise. The kid with the high-pitched voice who'd been so proud to report any small infraction to the teacher. Like who had snuck *Henry and Mudge Under the Yellow Moon* inside their science book so they could *pretend* to be reading about the parts of plants. (That sneaky reader would be me.)

But this was not about Melanie slacking off in science to read about the adventures of a great big dog. This was a brutal killing. Which Melanie, of course, could not have been involved in, but it just felt wrong not to tell Andy what I'd heard.

"Hey, look," I began. "I'm guessing you guys already know, but Elizabeth was saying that Melanie was late— like really, *really* late—to work our booth on the day of the Fling. And she seemed upset." I took a breath. "Melanie could never do the kind of thing someone did to Eloise. But, well, it just seemed wrong not to pass that along."

"I appreciate it. Yeah, we were aware, but she had a reason when we talked to her that day." Andy cleared his throat. "That, of course, doesn't clear her. It doesn't mean there weren't *other things* going on with her that night or that morning. But her story was confirmed." Ever so slightly, his lips turned up into an almost smile. "Hamster escape at the Spring Fling!" he said. "Hamster successfully located."

"Taffy Marie!" I said.

The little white ball of fur made her home in the children's section of the library near a display of hamster books, both fiction and nonfiction. During many weeks of the year, the children at Somerset Harbor Elementary were responsible for her care as part of their animal-sciences curriculum. On the day of the Fling, I had noticed Taffy Marie displayed in her cage at the elementary school table, where the children were selling homemade pet treats to raise money for field trips.

Melanie would indeed have gone a little bonkers once she heard that Taffy had escaped. She had confessed to me once that when the library was quiet in the evenings, she would tell the hamster all about her secret crushes and what she *really thought* of certain members of the library board.

"And I could almost swear she's listening with those great big eyes—and that she agrees with my assessments of the oh-so-boring board," she had told me with a laugh. "My confidante is a hamster, and I am not ashamed."

Now, Andy continued with his story. "One of the kids took her out to pet her and forgot to shut the cage," he said.

Fred, the officer who drove me home that day, had been on the scene, providing security for the festival. And he had jumped into action when the hamster set off to explore the wonders of the Merchants Guild Spring Fling.

"Fred said he was sure that little fur ball was destined for a new home beyond the Easton Ames Memorial Library," Andy said. "Because, do you know, Rue, how hard it is to locate an escapee when said escapee is small enough to fit into the palm of your hand?"

"Thank goodness someone found her. The kids would have been heartbroken."

"It was a miracle of sorts." Andy picked up his pace, noticing the crowd around the church, which was just ahead.

Apparently, the pet had found a comfy spot and was curled into a teacup at the community-engagement booth that was set up every year. Leaders of various social groups in town took turns greeting guests beneath a sign that proclaimed, "Welcome to Somerset Harbor: So Many Ways to Play. Find Your Place Today!" And brochures and displays were set out to promote activities and clubs.

"Did you say a teacup?" I asked Andy. "That is kind of precious, really."

"Oh, but not to Benita Knightly of the Ladies Tea Club," he said with a laugh.

When the napping hamster was discovered, Benita had been in the process of describing the speakers and deep friendships that were hallmarks of her group. "And we do everything with a touch of elegance!" she'd said, looking down to find the hamster sound asleep in a bone china teacup: Renaissance Gold by Wedgwood, Benita's own beloved pattern.

I had always thought Taffy Marie had the air of a fine lady; now that I thought about it, the teacup seemed to be more her style than a cage. She had, as the sign said, "Found Her Place."

"And Melanie, I guess, was looking too?"

"Oh, yes, she'd arrived to town by then and was looking everywhere," said Andy.

I thought about it for a moment. "Here's what I don't get," I said. "When she finally made it to the booth, she didn't say a word about chasing down a hamster. Elizabeth had no idea why on earth she was so late."

"Well, witnesses concur that it was Melanie who rushed over to the booth, with the cage in hand, to pick the hamster up," said Andy. "Maybe she was shaken up. My guess is that maybe after all of that, she didn't care to relive the trauma. Your friend there seemed to take it hard when we all were thinking the children's little pet was gone." He paused. "We're still looking at her, Rue, but there have been...developments as well. We are really hoping to wrap this thing up quickly. All of us in town want to make sure there is justice—for our Eloise."

By then, the steps to the church were just ahead. And since there was a crowd, we made our way inside, hoping to find seats.

We squeezed into a row about halfway toward the front; no surprise there was a crowd. A respectful silence filled the room until the long line of Endicotts filed into the sanctuary as the organ played. Then the pastor took his place. A small and wiry man somewhere in his forties, he gave the crowd a sad smile and began to describe the ways that Eloise had impacted those around her.

"I think many of us have framed maps in our homes from Olde World Treasures," he said as he looked around him, acknowledging the nods. "And *treasures* is a grand way to describe the merchandise Eloise and Greta found for us to enjoy." He smiled. "How I used to love the stories Eloise would tell to make the little paper places on her maps come alive. And, friends, do you know what? Even as a grown man, I *believed* in the magic Eloise Endicott insisted could be found along the pathways depicted in her maps."

He looked out over the crowd. "Since the tragic weekend that has passed, I've talked to a lot of people about those maps and Eloise. And I've heard tales of magic. Roger Allen's map—a fine map of our town—shows an old wishing well down the south path to Lake Mallard. Not the path we all take and have taken all our lives. Oh, no, I mean the overgrown one to the south, where you have to make your way very carefully across the brambles and the vines. But Eloise sold Roger's family more than just a map; she sold them an adventure." He leaned across the podium. "Eloise told Roger's children they'd find a wishing well where fairies gather if they pulled back some heavy growth behind a certain tree." He paused. "Now, I can't vouch for the fairies," he said with a wink, "but Roger's family found the well, and they left some fairy treats. Because one never knows."

An appreciative murmur moved throughout the crowd.

"And that's just one of the many stories I've heard this week about the maps from Olde World Treasures," said the pastor. "Because Eloise understood how to take the time to really look at the world around her. Eloise knew how to love the things most people have forgotten. She taught us how to *see*."

I caught Andy's eye, and he nodded and smiled softly. It was a perfect service—and so very Eloise.

Afterward, the Methodist ladies were providing sandwiches and salads in the church reception room. We made our way down the hall to peek in, but the line to greet the family was stretched around the room. I needed to get back to the bookstore soon, and Andy, I could tell, was anxious to deal with those "developments" he had mentioned earlier.

Did they have to do with Barney and the bloody shirt? (What the heck was up with that?) I had spotted the delivery man near the front of the service, and here he was again in line. He seemed to be in the middle of a long story he was telling to Anna Geary from Anna's Ice Cream Cone.

I caught a glimpse of Laurel huddled with her cousins as they spoke briefly to each mourner. I longed to say hello, but now might not be the time. Greta, in the center of the group, wearing a sharp blue suit, looked like she had aged ten years in the last few days.

"Why don't we head on back?" I said. "And tomorrow, I'll catch up with Laurel." Today, she would be distracted. Tomorrow, with the service over, the tragedy might start to sink in even more; she would need me then.

Andy glanced down at his phone. "Yeah, I think the best thing I can do for Eloise is to get back to work."

That's when I felt a hand on my back, and I wheeled around.

"Laurel!"

She grabbed me in a hug.

"I just can't say how sorry I am about Eloise," I said. "She was everybody's aunt. She adopted all of us!"

She held on a little longer. "Thank you for coming, Rue. They've kept us on an ordered schedule for the service and the burial and all—but I had to run over and say hi. It was good to look out in the crowd and see a friend."

When she let go, I could see her locking eyes with one of the cousins.

"Hey, I know you need to go," I said and squeezed her hand. "Let's catch up soon, okay? Are you in town for a while?"

She nodded tearfully, and then she was off—with the little half-hop and half-run that I remembered from all those summers long ago.

It wasn't until she was gone that I looked down at my hand to find a slip of paper folded into a tiny square—another memory from my childhood summers.

Slowly, I unfolded it.

"LH. 4 p.m. tomorrow. RC and LE"

The lighthouse—or LH—in those days was her go-to place when there was drama to discuss or when (more times than not) "LE" was in trouble and needed rescuing by "RC." But best not to spell things out in writing. Because, you see, according to Laurel in those days, there were always spies or pirates who might intercept a note. And there were those pesky trolls who hung out by the bay.

But there was safety at the lighthouse, where we could settle in on our special bench that overlooked the sea. There, we always managed to figure it all out.

Now our hearts were broken. But maybe at LH, the healing could begin.

CHAPTER NINE

The next day we did a steady business at the store. In the few quiet moments when we could catch our breath, we shared our thoughts about the service.

Carole had ended up sitting next to Barney at the luncheon, and he had given her an earful about the day before, when two cops stopped by his house.

Always the optimist, the poor old man at first had misunderstood the nature of the "little chat" that they proposed. He assumed the guys were there to check on his well-being and seek out his ideas to keep the town as safe as possible for the senior population.

"Oh, no. He thought that, really?" Elizabeth winced and buried her head in her hands.

"Oh, yeah, he did," said Carole, brushing some red

curls off of her forehead. "He was confused when the officers began to just go on and on about that awful business with poor Eloise."

"I can just imagine. That would frighten me to death," said Elizabeth.

"Then the poor man imagined they must want his opinion on *how to investigate a murder.* Which would just be insane," Carole continued with the story. "You know, Barney doesn't even watch those crime shows on TV that are so popular these days. *Happy* endings are his thing. So what would an old bug man know about that stuff?" She paused, taking a breath as though she was preparing herself to utter her next words. "Then they asked him where he was when Eloise was killed. They even wanted fingerprints from Barney."

"Oh, no." Elizabeth covered her chin with her fingers. "I bet he was shocked."

"He was appalled. He even went as far as to present them with a list of his community involvements and told them they were wrong about what kind of man he is. Then he asked them to leave."

"That's so odd," I said. "No way was it Barney."

"That's what I was thinking," said Elizabeth as she straightened up some books. "He used to come to my house four times a year to spray for bugs. And I honestly used to think the guy was too tenderhearted to even do his job. Once he had to spray to get rid of ants—and he *apologized* to the creepy little things. Said he felt like he was killing a whole town of bugs."

Carole rolled her eyes. "Once I asked him to knock down a cobweb on my porch, and he just looked forlorn. Said it was a shame he had to destroy *such a delicate endeavor.*" Then she paused dramatically. "But...the cops eventually told Barney why they were *really there.*"

"Carole!" I set down my cup of tea. This story was like one of those maddening books that only gets exciting at the very end.

"Well, why did you save that part for last? Tell us what they said." Elizabeth's eyes were wide.

"They found a bloody shirt in the bed of Barney's truck!" said Carole breathlessly. "While they were on the scene the morning of the murder! He had parked his truck behind the florist's shop. Because there is a spot there that's reserved for him when he's picking up his flowers for deliveries. And we all know how parking is when there's something big in town. So he just parked it there and walked over to the Fling."

I gasped. "But surely someone besides Barney threw that thing in there." Since the florist's was right there beside Eloise's, the truck bed might have seemed to be a quick and easy place for the murderer to "lose the evidence" if he (or she) escaped behind the store.

Carole shrugged. "Yeah. Surely no one really thinks it's Barney. But I guess they have to ask since it was his truck. Police procedure, I suppose."

About an hour later, I grabbed Gatsby's leash, and we headed to the lighthouse, a black and white structure that was often seen on T-shirts and postcards that were snapped up eagerly by tourists. All of Somerset Harbor seemed to be in bloom, and Gatsby constantly pulled at his leash to sniff the bright blossoms in yellow, pink, and red.

He got even more excited when he understood we were going to the beach. And, as we got closer to the lighthouse, there was Laurel, squatting down to greet him as he strained at his leash. I let him off the lead for just a moment, as there was no way I could fly toward Laurel as fast as Gatsby would have pulled me had I not let him go.

He had only met her once during one of her visits home, but she'd made an impression. Possibly because she was my only human friend who loved to chase and run and catch as much as Gatsby did.

"Look at you!" she cried as he licked her face. "Aren't you the handsome boy?" Then she stood to greet me with a hug. "Thanks for coming, Rue. I needed me some Rue time."

I secured Gatsby's leash back onto his collar. "I just can't imagine how unbelievably horrific this whole week has been," I said.

Then we both smiled at Gatsby, who was whirling around in delighted circles, still beside himself with joy.

"On the plus side," I told Laurel, "you just made someone's day."

We walked toward the red bench where we always liked to sit. In my opinion, it was the best meeting spot in town—with a view of both the lighthouse and the water.

"So. How are you, really, Laurel?" I asked, sitting down.

"Still in shock," she said. "And you know how you always think that families come together in a crisis? Well, Rue, I don't know. With the family, it's weird."

Yes, it was very weird. But as far as Laurel was concerned, all of that was news to me.

"What's going on?" I asked.

"I mean, can't we all just mourn our aunt during *this one visit* and forget the other stuff for a few days at least?" She let out a sigh. "It's not like any of my cousins are so hard up for money we have to decide right now who inherits what. And my dad is pretty sure the wills were set up long ago so that everything would go to either Eloise or Greta, whichever one was left. And then they would be the one to distribute their estate."

I touched Laurel's hand. "That must be so hurtful to see them focusing on that. The loss of Eloise is huge—impossible almost." I paused. "So, is there some 'golden item' everybody wants to grab? What exactly is the deal?"

In other words, why is everybody fighting over the Newcastle map?

"They all want to get their hands on a map, if you can believe it." My friend spoke in a whisper, even though no one was around but me and her. "And, Rue, what no one knows is that Aunt Eloise wanted it to go to *me*—or I'm almost sure she did. Because she told me—and only me—the *secret* of the map."

My heart skipped a beat. "There's a secret to the map?"

Laurel had not outgrown her tendency to embellish, to infuse drama into a quick trip to the store to grab some bread and soda. But I'd heard for myself that the cousins *also* felt there was something about the map—something that made each of them want to get their hands on it.

"There's another map below it!" Laurel breathed. "Of

Snapdragon Lane, where Aunt grew up. Right here in Somerset."

I glanced at her, confused. "But why would she hide that?"

My friend stroked Gatsby's back. "She made a promise to her grandad it would be their little secret, just between the two of them. He was the one who drew the map—as a surprise for her when she was six years old. And not long after that, he died. So even when she grew up, it was her little piece of him: the secrets of the map."

"Secrets such as…"

"Like where the leprechauns liked to go to dance out beyond the garden. There was a leprechaun named Jack who was the slowest of the bunch and always a bad hider. So, her grandad would help Aunt Eloise put out cheese and crackers as a lure, hoping he'd come out."

So far, this wasn't a story that could get a person murdered—but it nonetheless was sweet.

"Coolest ever grandpa," I said. "Do leprechauns supposedly like cheese and crackers?"

Laurel shrugged. "Doesn't everyone? I think she liked the idea that they still had a secret, even after he was gone."

"That makes sense," I said. "She mentioned him a few times when I was in the store."

"I think she got her love of stories and her love of maps from him. She and Greta both. She told me that she'd take the map out of the frame sometimes when she was by herself and just look at it for a while—at all of her climbing trees and the houses of her friends on her childhood street." Laurel flipped her hair over her shoulder.

It was a charming story, but I was still confused. "So, what exactly is the deal with the Newcastle map?" I asked. "Why are all the cousins fighting over that one—if they have no idea what else is in the frame?"

"Eloise loved that one, which is why she picked it to put in the frame with her other special map. It was her favorite trip—to Newcastle upon Tyne when she was in her twenties. And some of her best stories were about the map—with the fortress and the bell tower and all the other places that she loved."

That still did not explain it. A sentimental favorite, sure, for the family group—but it's not as if they were doing battle over a signed Picasso. Something was missing from this story—an important piece.

Gatsby whined a little and barked at some birds overhead; he was getting restless.

"How about a walk?" I asked.

Gatsby barked an enthusiastic yes.

Laurel scratched behind his ears. "She was talking to me, silly, but I agree with you." She stood up. "Let's go."

"Did you ever see the other map, of her old neighborhood?" I asked as we started down the rocky pathway to the beach.

"Oh, man, I wish I had. But one time when I was sick —I was eight or so, I guess—she was doing everything she could to try to cheer me up. And she knew me well enough to know my very favorite thing was to know a secret. And that's when I heard the story of her 'secret map.' That way, I could know a little something the others didn't know—since I was missing so much fun." She let out a sigh. "What a bummer of a summer, Rue. I missed *three* birthday parties. It was awful! Not to mention having to stay home on the couch on the Fourth of July—when there were fireworks on the beach."

"I remember that! I brought you a favor bag that year from Paula Engel's party. The theme was unicorns."

What was funny at the time was that the tough and street-smart Laurel had still believed in unicorns. Even sheltered little Rue knew the candy-colored flying creatures were a made-up thing. And even now, the grown-up Laurel was a crazy mix of tough and gullible. She'd gone on to run her own successful all-natural pet food brand, managing a staff with great insight and practicality along with a budget and supplies and everything that went with running one's own business. And yet she still believed in things that most of us at our age could see through in a heartbeat. She thought every infomercial might just change her life, that each gossipy headline told some amazing truth about the stars of her favorite TV shows.

"It's kind of cool," I said, "that she shared all of that with you—so that the secret could live on with the next generation."

"Oh! And her grandpa also told her there was pirate treasure buried on the east side of the lawn, the side closest to the sea, and he marked the spot with a drawing of a coin. And he drew a little teacup in the spot where she used to have her parties with her dolls." Laurel gave me a small smile. "And she kind of hinted she might go out and hide a little something for me in the spot with the picture of the teacup. To look for when I was older." She paused. "That is another reason that I'm sure the map was meant for me."

Eloise and Greta had lived on the property well into their fifties. Then their worsening eyesight made it more convenient for them to live above their shop for a quick commute. An uncle lived there now along with a cousin.

"But everybody else—they're that intent on getting

their hands on a map of some random place Eloise once went to on vacation?"

"I know! It's so stupid, right?" Then she narrowed her eyes. "Sometimes, Rue, I really wonder if they know about the other map—and, you know, the treasure."

"You mean the *pirate treasure?* The thing about her grandpa—and how he drew the map for her—that would make that map kind of special to everyone, I guess. If they knew the map was there." Not that these cousins seemed to be a sentimental bunch.

"Maybe that's the reason they claim to want the Newcastle map, to get to the one beneath it," Laurel said thoughtfully. She stopped walking and looked me in the eye. "Do you think they know? About the pirate treasure?"

"But it's a treasure from a story! It's not like there's a bunch of gold that's really buried in the yard."

"But there were pirates *right here,* Rue. Pirates—they were real."

Was she even serious?

"Well, yeah, they were here. But real pirates would have spent their gold on rum and on having a good time. Don't you think the whole buried-treasure bit is kind of more like a fiction thing?"

"Well, maybe these were practical kinds of pirates, the kind who liked to save." Laurel shrugged.

Okay, I give up, I thought.

"What is next for Greta? Will she run the shop alone?" I was curious to see if Laurel was aware of Greta's plans to sell. And how she might explain it, since Eloise had seemed determined to keep things as they had always been.

Laurel frowned. "Well. Some of my more money-hungry cousins seem determined she should sell—and they've thought that for a while. The building's worth a lot, and I guess they've got their eye on the money they'll get one day in her will. My cousin Jared, even, did some research on what improvements to the building would help her get top price. And last year, he typed out a list of suggestions for Aunt Eloise and Aunt Greta! Who, mind you, had no intention of putting their shop on the market. Jared only wants to open up a bike shop and he doesn't have the sense to get the funds all on his own. So he wants his money now from the sale of the shop. How selfish can you get?"

"Did they consider selling?"

"Not Aunt Eloise. No way. She would have been lost without the shop. Now, Aunt Greta on the other hand? I think she was more than ready to do some traveling and just be done with work. I think the two of them had some 'talks' that weren't exactly pleasant. Each of them felt strongly that they should sell—or stay. But as long as

Aunt Eloise wanted to stay put, Aunt Greta had decided that's what they should do—always the big sister."

Or had Greta at some point decided something else?

Laurel kicked off her red tennis shoes as we got closer to the beach, and I slipped out of my flats.

"But Jared's up to something, and that boy has some nerve," said Laurel. "You won't believe what I found at that shop. You know that little corner with the couches —that they call the Sit and Sip?"

That was the name Eloise had given the area with the antique camelback sofas, where she would sit and visit with customers and where they could flip through the vintage books or the latest copies of antiquing magazines. Like we did at the Seabreeze, Eloise kept a selection of fine teas to serve to guests. All good and well in the bookshop, where guests weren't seated on extravagantly priced furniture that we hoped to eventually sell. I could tell that gave Greta fits, but Eloise always said good furniture was meant to be enjoyed.

"Yeah, I know the Sit and Sip," I said. I myself had sat and sipped—very carefully.

"Well, when we were going through some things at the store, I found an envelope with Aunt Greta's name on one of the tables there. It was an envelope from Jared." Laurel picked up a stick of driftwood to throw out for Gatsby. "Inside were a bunch of papers about this idea he has for a bike shop. Like, he was pushing her to sell by showing how he'd spend the money if he could live out 'his dream' and support his little boys." Laurel rolled her eyes. "You know that when you mention any of the little ones, that will get to our Aunt Greta."

"Not the finest branch of your family tree," I said. Had he also tried to win over Eloise and failed? How far would he have gone after that?

Gatsby flew back with the driftwood, and Laurel threw the stick again. "And here's the thing about it, Rue. Jared never sticks to any plan at once. Just the other day, he wanted to get *bees* and start a honey business."

With a start, I remembered the brochures stuck under the door the day I found the body: beekeeping, home brewing, and spelunking.

"Caves! Does he like exploring caves? And making his own beer?"

Laurel looked confused. "*What?* No! I don't think so, Rue." She paused to think. "I don't think any of us cousins will be making our own beer. Because of that florist guy—the one who is a dentist? Who has the store next to my aunts? That guy dabbles in home brewing. One day we all were at the store, and he brought some of his beer to us. And that stuff was so bad, I think all of us have sworn off that as a hobby."

"Yeah, Dennis. He's my dentist. I've been seeing him a lot." I grimaced. "Wisdom teeth."

"Yeah, Dennis. That guy likes to talk. You know, I think he might have been the one who talked the bee thing up to Jared."

"Dennis is into that?"

Hmm. How many people in this town would have an interest in both beekeeping and home brewing? Had *Dennis* been the one who had grabbed those three brochures on the morning of the murder? With a failing business, surely not. Who had time to brew and keep bees and all of that?

But, still, my dentist *had* been acting strangely.

I was starting to feel unsettled. About so many people. About so many things.

CHAPTER TEN

The next day was unseasonably cool. Having a half-day off in the afternoon, I whipped up a batch of Gran's chicken gumbo soup. She had left the recipe for me along with the big pot handed down to her by her own gran. Until I had my wisdom teeth removed in ten days, it would be a bit of soft deliciousness that wouldn't make me scream with pain.

And best of all, I could take some to Greta. Most of the family, Laurel had told me, were clearing out today. And the few who remained were staying at Captain Jack's Bed and Breakfast before they headed out in a few more days. During her first night alone in the apartment, Greta might find some comfort in a friendly face.

I had spoken to Andy briefly on the phone as I walked to work that morning, tipping off my friend about the greedy-cousin twist. He said something vague about how the cops had become aware of some "family money pressure," and I left it at that.

As I cut up some celery, I thought about that map everyone was after. What was up with that?

Laurel had said she was the only one Eloise had told about the map beneath the map. But I suspected she was wrong. Eloise, you see, had a way of making everyone feel special—like every single one of us who loved her was the "only one," each in our own way.

Was there a "secret" hidden on the map for each of the cousins? An idea planted in each brain by Eloise so they could one day find the kind of hidden treasures the pastor had described? Maybe Eloise had felt they could discover things together if there was just one map for them all. A family treasure hunt that would keep the cousins close.

Ah. Little had she known how wrong that plan would go—if that indeed had been the plan.

It was a little before six when I climbed the steps to Greta's apartment above the store. When I rapped on her door, I could hear shuffling footsteps. "On my way," she called out. "I'm a little slow."

When she opened the door to me, her eyes lit up, although I could tell they were red from crying. "Rue! How sweet of you to visit, and whatever you have brought me smells divine." Even in her grief, her blouse was ironed, and her short gray hair was all in place.

I kissed her papery thin cheek. "I won't stay for long. I know this week must have been exhausting. Oh, Greta, I'm so sorry."

"Well, people have been kind. Did you know that *every single day* Sissie would tell me how blessed we were to live here? And she was absolutely right. Come in and take a seat. What can I get you, dear?"

"Not a thing besides your company, then I'll let you rest." I slipped into the kitchen to set the soup container on the stove, then I joined Greta in the den. The small, neat room was furnished with high-end pieces, and I settled onto a dark green velvet couch covered in gold pillows.

"I hope you got to spend some time with Laurel." Greta shook her head. "The two of you together could be trouble way back when you were young." She gave me a wink.

"But we had a good time." I smiled. "I'd like to think today I behave more properly."

"Laurel, Laurel, Laurel! In a lot of ways, I do believe that she's the smartest of the bunch," said Greta. "But if I told her a flying pig had landed in the yard, she'd run to the fridge to fix the thing a snack."

"That she would." I laughed.

In the silence that followed that, I noticed *Oliver Twist* among some books that had been arranged just so around a Waterford Crystal vase on the coffee table.

Well, wasn't that just perfect. One of the delicate topics I wanted to bring up was Melanie's visits to the store—and here was my chance.

"I named my little white cat after the boy in that book," I said. "Because my Ollie also seemed to be an orphan in need of a home. And also, when I fed him, he always wanted more. Like Dickens's Oliver."

She looked down at Magellan, who was showing off his ample tummy as he lay on the carpet. "Yes, this one loves his food as well—as everyone can see."

"Are you reading that with Melanie? Because one of her clubs this year is doing Dickens."

Greta sighed. "Oh, I am aware. But I think I would prefer to just read on my own."

"Oh, yeah? I hear they have some good discussions, and they would love to have you."

Greta leaned back in her chair. "Well, my sister was more of a 'joiner' than I am. Plus, that young librarian... well, she is rather pushy, don't you think?"

"Yeah, she can be a lot, but she means well, Greta." I paused. "Did something happen between you and Melanie? If you don't mind me asking."

Greta lifted her hands and let them fall on the

armrests. "Oh, my goodness, Rue. She came into the store, wanting to borrow this and that—things to do with England in Dickens's time, you see. She had the grand idea to 'sex up' the classics—that is how she put it —with a big display to advertise her club. She was hoping to encourage readers to pick up the masters and not just today's bestsellers. Which I can support, although my taste runs more to Austen or Mark Twain. Dickens can be bleak."

"And was she acting pushy with you or Eloise?"

"Oh, you know how Sissie was. She would have given her the moon! Anything for her beloved Somerset. And we had set aside some stuff to let Melanie display— nice, attention-getting items. And with some hefty price tags, I might add. I knew there was some risk an item might get stolen. But this community has been good to us, and we've always done our part."

"You have."

"And then there was the business of the candlestick."

"The candlestick?"

Greta nodded to where it sat, tall and elegant, on a table in the corner. "You see, dear, it was his."

"His?"

Greta nodded solemnly.

When I still looked confused, she nodded to the book.

"*His?* As in *Him?* As in *Charles Dickens?*"

"It was Dickens's candlestick."

I was glad I didn't have a drink to drop onto the expensive couch.

"We have, of course, a letter of authenticity. And a photograph of him working at his desk with the item in the background."

I could barely breathe. Dickens was absolutely one of my top-five favorite writers. He could have written *Great Expectations*—or conjured up Ebenezer Scrooge— by the light of the very candlestick that was *six feet away from me.*

"Melanie," my host continued, "thought it appropriate to display the candlestick at the library, but Eloise and I agreed we could not do that. I thought about it for one night, but I was plagued with nightmares of that thing disappearing out the door underneath a jacket."

Magellan landed in my lap with a thud, and I stroked his fur after I got over the surprise of the incoming pet; I was used to lighter felines, but Magellan was a sweetie.

"Melanie, I take it, did not respond well to the no?" I asked.

How unlike Melanie—who should have understood the enormity of what she was asking from the sisters.

"Apparently, she's under pressure from the board to increase the number of adult visitors to the facility," said

Greta. "And she tries to do so much with such a little budget. But apparently, she took all her frustration out on Sissie, and for that, I cannot forgive her, Rue. The things she said to my sister—on more than one occasion—were unspeakable."

"How horrible for Eloise—and after all the things that both of you have done for the library and for all of us."

Magellan let out a sad meow as if he agreed.

"She was even worse than Dennis." Then Greta's hand flew to her mouth. "Oh, dear, I should hush. Talking about people! I hope you will forgive me. A broken heart, it seems, loosens an old woman's tongue. But grief is no excuse for me to forget my manners."

"Sometimes I think it's good to just get your feelings out," I said. I prided myself on being a good confidante, which I would be to Greta—unless, of course, I heard something I should pass on to Andy. "As much as I like Dennis," I continued, "I imagine that it can't be easy having him around so much—the way he loves to talk, and with his shop right next door."

"Well, we'll see how long that lasts. We've helped him with the rent a few times, but we can only do so much. I don't know how much longer the landlord will let him stay."

"Oh, so it's *that bad?*"

"I'm afraid it is. And at times he seems so desperate. He's asked us to sell some of his old knickknacks in the store—like we are some pawn shop. And he asked if we would pay his wife to come in and dust. Although how fair would that have been to the young lady who has cleaned for us for years?"

"Well, I hate to hear that, Greta."

"And please, Rue, just keep that to yourself. Dennis is a fine man who has fallen on hard times. That new florist on Elm and March Street has really hurt his business. And a good many families here have switched to that new, young dentist who goes to church with us." She let out a sigh. "I do hope he finds his way."

I was already tense, and my mind began to spin. Had he turned to theft, and had things gone wrong? But, no! As my host had said about herself, my mind should just hush and not think nasty things.

About that time, Greta's phone rang.

"Should you get that?" I pointed my eyes at the old-fashioned landline.

"Oh, no. That would be my nephew Jared, who calls day and night. It seems he has decided that I am too old to run my own life for myself." She paused. "I have made some decisions, Rue, that would have not pleased my sister. Over the last month, Jared has been helping me put some things in place to allow us to retire. Or I guess

I should say the process has begun. Selling our building here would, of course, have required the signature of Eloise. Sissie was determined we would never sell, but I felt the time had come. And I planned to broach the subject again with my sister and try to convince her one more time." Her voice began to quiver. "I hate we were at odds during the last weeks of her life."

I reached out to touch her hand. "No one could have had a better sister than you were to Eloise."

"Not long before she died, I said to Jared I could not continue making plans to sell as long as the idea of a sale hurt my sister like it did. If she said no again, then we were staying put." Absently, she smoothed out a wrinkle in her slacks.

The landline rang again, and Greta glared at it. "Now, he is determined that the time is ripe—and with my sister barely in the ground. But now I am not so sure I even want to sell. Because down there in my shop, I can sense my sister with me."

"Well, it's your decision, Greta. Don't let him pressure you."

As Magellan nuzzled my arm, I stroked his fur and made a mental note to learn more about this Jared.

CHAPTER ELEVEN

I woke up the next morning with my mind in a jumble. So many theories—and a zillion questions—were competing in my head for space. It had made it hard to sleep.

To start, there was Jared, who seemed almost *crazed* in his grab for money to open up his shop. But as long as Eloise and her "no" vote were around, he knew that Olde World Treasures would not be going up for sale.

Dennis, shockingly, was another one who was desperate to get money. And where else in town could one find such an array of pricey things to resell on the black market when bills were overdue and cash was short? That bloody shirt, after all, had been found behind the florist shop he owned.

But *my own dentist?* Shoving that sword in my friend's chest? My mind could not go there.

And some things about the murder still made no sense to me. Like, how did *no one see the killer,* who had to have been all bloody? If the coroner had it right, someone had killed Eloise during the Spring Fling—or at least while workers were setting up their booths. But that couldn't be! With the back door locked up tight, how did someone exit out the *front door* in front of all those people? And then lose the bloody shirt all the way *behind* the building and a little to the right, where Barney's pickup truck was parked behind Kramer's Florist?

It all just made my head hurt.

But the pounding at my temples was a spa day with a hot-stone massage compared to the sharp pain in my jaw. Things in my mouth were rapidly getting worse.

Speaking of my dentist, I wondered if there was any way he could move my procedure up—like maybe to today. Because…well, just *ouch.*

That would, of course, be complicated. Dennis had explained to me that after the wisdom teeth came out, I would have to take it easy for a day or two. And that would mean asking Elizabeth and Carole to put in some extra hours—with very little notice.

Still, this searing pain seemed like an emergency, and it had put me in a mood.

I got up and made coffee, then I called the dentist's office as soon as I thought they would be open.

Ethel answered cheerfully. Dennis would not be in till noon, she said, but I could come in at 1:15. And, yes, my wisdom teeth could indeed come out today as opposed to next week as scheduled.

"You're in luck!" she said.

I suspected it was more about empty schedules with so many customers apparently abandoning the practice for the "new and shiny" dentist. But I was relieved to get in early and end this torture ASAP.

"Thank goodness," I told Ethel.

She reminded me about no heavy meals because of the local anesthesia.

Since I couldn't chew, that wouldn't be a problem.

"See you soon," I said.

A little later at the Seabreeze, things were fairly busy. Elizabeth had given me her blessing to do what I had to do to get my mouth in shape, and I spent the morning making sure things were in order for me to miss a day or two.

When I got a break, I sent a text to Laurel to see what her schedule was like for the next few days. I really hoped the two of us could get one more visit in before she got out of town. Not that I would be the most fun companion. But maybe we could sit out on my porch while I held an ice pack to my mouth.

I was straightening some clothbound journals when I heard someone step up beside me.

"That one with the birds is nice. Such soothing muted colors—like Monet might have drawn a blue and yellow bird." I looked up to see Irene from Papa's Seafood standing next to me.

"I love this line of journals," I told her with a smile. "And there's a pocket on the inside of the cover in the back."

"Well, then I have to have it." She put it in her basket. "It just relieves the stress to pour my words out on the page."

"A journal listens to you," I said with a nod. "Unlike a lot of humans," I added with a laugh. "And we guarantee none of our journals will talk back to customers and tell them their life choices are all wrong." I studied the flowery branches the birds were perched upon. "Seriously, though, we all need the stress release. Hasn't this just been the most heartbreaking week?"

Irene dropped her voice to a whisper. "That bloody shirt from Barney's truck? They confirmed yesterday that the blood was Eloise's. No big surprise, I guess, but hopefully that will bring us closer to having somebody locked up."

"Eloise's blood? How do you know that?"

"One of the evidence techs was in the restaurant last night—for our fried-shrimp special. And since there was also a special on rum punch, his lips got a little loose."

"Interesting," I said with a nod that sent a searing pain through my jaw.

I struggled through the morning till I left for the dentist. I got to the parking lot at Dennis's just in time to see Melanie exiting the office. She looked as miserable as me.

"Teeth!" I joked with a weary smile. "Why can't they just do their job and *chew* and not go all rebellious on us?"

"I know! Right? What's going on with you?" she asked.

"Wisdom teeth. And you?"

"Well, apparently, I grind my teeth when I'm stressed. So now I have to get a mouthguard. Because the stress right now is through the roof—like to the max and beyond." She leaned against my car and sighed.

"Oh, Mel. I'm so sorry."

"I swear, this library board this year is straight out of Dante's nine circles of...well, you-know-where. Rue, they are the worst. They're all about pleasing certain people who are the biggest donors. They think I 'waste' my time on 'low-profile' stuff like the children's programs. Which people absolutely love!"

"Okay, that's just nuts. Those programs build their base of readers." Not to mention teaching children if they always have a book, they'll never be alone.

"And when it comes to the adults, they're all about the numbers: how many bodies we have walking through the door, if we meet their standards of books checked out per week. Never mind how enthusiastic people are about our book clubs and our programs. They just don't get it, Rue: that it's never about numbers when it comes to books. If you can open up *one* mind, then that makes it a good day."

"Absolutely." I always thought the library—and the Seabreeze—made our town that much smarter.

"One of the big donors is obsessed with Dickens. So I was really hoping if we could build up the numbers in the classics reading group, the board might come around and be more supportive. But nothing seems to work when it comes to that. It's a great group of readers. We have the best discussions! But the board just sees the *numbers*." She ran her fingers through her hair. "Not that it's my *teeth's* fault! But, Dennis tells me I'm a champ when it comes to grinding my poor teeth."

"Well, I hate to hear it. I had no idea things were that bad with the board."

"I'm kind of scared about my job, to be honest with you. And then this thing with Eloise! With all those questions that officer was throwing at me—it was like he thought I was the one who hurt her, which kind of freaked me out." She paused. "And Rue…" She looked down at the pavement. "One day I had kind of had it, and I took it out on Eloise. And for that, I cannot forgive myself."

I looked her in the eye and saw tears pooling there. "That was one bad moment among a million moments when you make people's day. They're always coming in the bookstore to say you introduced them to an author —and now they're coming in to buy everything she's written. They are begging me to know when something new is coming out. You are the book whisperer, Mel. You just keep doing what you do."

"Thanks." She gave me a weak smile. "Good luck with the teeth."

I looked at the door. "The sooner I walk in there, the sooner this thing will be over."

She touched my arm for courage, and then I was off.

Once I got inside the office, Ethel gave me a sympathetic smile. "It never is as bad as people think it will be. Onward, ninja, fight!" It was our rallying cry when we were part of the same summer girl gang when I would visit Gran. Mostly, it was what we said when one of Laurel's dangerous ideas was about to get us all in trouble.

Kara appeared next and took me straight back to Dennis. "You've had a rough time these last few weeks," she said, "but this will get you back to feeling normal, and normal will feel awesome, right?"

Dennis was lining up his tools, and he gave me a smile as I got into the chair. "Well, if it's not my favorite seller of fine books!" he said as he perched beside me on a stool. "I know this is a day you've dreaded, but this is a good decision, Rue. The recovery won't be bad. And in addition to getting rid of the pain you're feeling now, this will eliminate a lot of future problems with your teeth."

Hmm. He was sounding more like someone else's dentist: matter-of-fact and optimistic. And missing the very obvious bad joke about no more *wisdom* teeth. He just seemed...very different.

Despite the pain in my mouth—and my nerves about anything having to do with being in the dentist's chair—my mind pinged back to the murder. "Hey, Dennis, by the way, what do you think of Laurel's cousin Jared? You've met Jared, right?"

Dennis made a face. "What do I think of him? Not

much. Even as a little kid, he was a sneaky one. And greedy as the day is long. Used to come in here when I was just starting out. He'd strut over to the treat box we keep for the kids, and he'd stuff one or two of the prizes in his pocket when he thought no one could see. Then he'd smile all cocky-like and hold his hand out for another. But that little hooligan wasn't fooling anyone."

That sounded about right.

"Hasn't changed much since those days." Dennis got me fixed up with a bib and picked up one of his tools.

The procedure took about thirty minutes and, with some light sedation, I just felt a little pressure, nothing more. Dennis continued to be...well, not very Dennis-like. Instead of garrulous and loud, he was quiet and distracted.

I let out a sigh of relief when he announced, "Wisdom teeth all gone!" The ordeal was through, and hopefully, the process of recovery wouldn't be too bad.

"You see, Rue? You did fine."

Over-the-counter meds might work for the pain, he said, but he gave me a prescription for something stronger just in case. I figured I would need it. When it came to dental stuff, I could be a wimp.

I thanked him and was heading to the desk to pay when I heard my phone ding. I pulled it from my purse to see that it was Laurel texting back. What a long string of words, I thought. Whether in person or through texts, she always had a lot to say.

I clicked on the text and read while Ethel pulled up my account on the computer.

"Would love to see you, Rue," Laurel had written. "But I need to head back soon. I honestly woke up hoping I could get out of here today. Not that I wouldn't love to stay in Somerset Harbor for the week! But there is some craziness, it seems, breaking out at work." That was followed by a frowny-face emoji. "But wouldn't you just know it? I stopped by the antique shop and left my purse inside! So, no car keys and no wallet. And now Greta's napping, and she has both keys to the shop. Plus, I need to run by the frame shop and do some other errands before I can leave town. And Greta's naps can be kind of epic. When she lays down for a nap, she can be out for a while."

I guessed the shop was closed today. Greta had never been one for keeping normal hours, and the shop had been closed a lot this week while she mourned her sister and spent time with her family.

Hmm. Laurel had no car to run her errands. Plus, she had quite a drive and chaos back at home with her pet food business. As a fellow business owner, I could feel for Laurel.

"How did it go?" asked Ethel, looking up.

"So far, so good," I said, still looking at my phone. "But Laurel's in a mess. Because…well, she's Laurel."

Ethel rolled her eyes and laughed. "What did she do this time?"

I told her about the purse and the thwarted plans Laurel had to leave.

Kara was lingering beside the desk. Seemingly, she didn't have a lot to do. The business seemed so quiet and so empty; it was really kind of sad.

"Oh, we can get Laurel into the shop. No problem!" Kara waved her hand. "Dennis has a key."

"He does? He has a key? To Olde World Treasures?" My earlier suspicions moved into high gear. The facts scrolled through my mind: the brochures at the crime scene about the activities he'd been known to enjoy. The way he'd lied to me that day about why he was on the sidewalk outside the antique shop. The desperate need for money.

It did, of course, make sense he would have a key. He was close to Greta and had been close to Eloise as well. Since he had been a trusted neighbor of the store for decades, he could hold onto a key in case one of theirs was lost. Or he could get into the shop in case of an emergency while they were away.

But it also seemed *the killer had a key,* which was a thought that chilled me. Someone with a key could have gone out the back and locked the door behind him, out of sight from those who were enjoying the Spring Fling.

"Hey!" I was startled by Dennis's booming voice. "Did I hear Laurel needs to get into the store?" he asked. "I have the keys right here."

In his hand was a leather key chain with two keys: presumably one for the front of the antique shop and—most importantly—one for the back as well.

CHAPTER TWELVE

I tried not to jump to conclusions. There were two things I could do, and I would calmly do those things.

I could get Laurel on her way, off to her work emergency. And I could update Andy, who most likely would *not* pick up the phone unless it was someone from work. But, luckily, his private investigations office was not far from the dentist's. I would try him there.

I texted Laurel first. "Great news! I was at the dentist's, and Dennis has a key. Meet you in thirty minutes at Olde World Treasures?"

The answer came back right away: a smiling emoji. "Rue, you are amazing. See you at the shop."

Then I walked to Andy's office, which was practically across the street. He and Dennis had both set up their offices about ten minutes from downtown in the non-touristy part of Somerset Harbor, where locals went to do a lot of their business.

I climbed up the wooden steps to the restored private home with the discreet sign on the door that read, "Prestige Investigations." In smaller letters, it said, "Experienced, Thorough, Confidential."

I hoped none of his private clients had emergencies this week; I had a feeling Andy was going hard on *the* investigation on a full-time basis.

As I let myself in, he was standing at his desk shouting into the phone. "How in the blazes can they tell us we don't have enough to make the arrest right now? We need to do it yesterday!" He looked furious when he hung up, and that was not like Andy. He was often frazzled, sometimes a little grumpy, but he was slow to lose his temper.

"Sounds like you're getting close," I said, slipping into his office.

"I *think* so. At least I am hoping. We need to get this done." He rubbed at his forehead, then he looked at me, concerned. "Hey, you okay there, Rue?"

"I have fewer wisdom teeth than when I woke up today. Which explains why I was just across the street."

"Ah, I see. I hear that can be rough. Can I help in any way?"

"So far, I'm okay, but perhaps *I* can help *you*."

That made him look even more exhausted; he was not a fan of my help with his investigations. "Rue, we have it handled. Please go home and rest, which I'm sure they told you to do across the street." He let out a sigh. "I'm kind of in a rush to get a few things handled over here. Things are moving forward, but, well, to be honest with you, I have a big concern. I'm concerned a major suspect may pull a disappearing act if we don't get some things in place to move in for an arrest. Because there are indications that...we may need to hurry."

Now, *that* was interesting.

"I understand," I said. "So I shouldn't trouble you with my new information—about who has a key to the back door of Eloise and Greta's shop?"

Andy's eyes grew huge. "That's pretty major, Rue. How exactly did..."

So. He had it handled, huh?

I sat down in the chair across from his desk. "It's interesting, Andy, the things a patient can find out just settling a bill at the dentist." I paused for a moment. "Dennis had the keys. He's apparently had them for forever."

Andy frowned. "I could have sworn we asked all the nearby merchants about an extra key. And we asked

Greta too, but it might have been so long ago that she gave him one, she might have forgotten."

"There's been a lot on Greta's mind."

He nodded. "And Dennis might have chosen to keep that info from the cops. Some people like to keep things to themselves if they think it will make them look at all suspicious. You know, like easy access to the murder site." He sunk down into his desk chair. "Not that we would think it odd for the Endicotts to have given him a key. It just makes sense, I guess, for him to keep one for his neighbors. But in this particular case..." He paused, deep in thought. "This is very helpful, Rue."

"Oh, yes, it could be key," I said. "Which is kind of a bad Dennis joke when you think about it. You know—key and *key?*"

Andy responded with a grunt.

"Sorry. That was bad."

Andy ran his hand over his head. "So...he just up and *told you* that he had a key?"

"Well, you see, a family member needed to get in, and Greta, it seems, is asleep." I paused. "So this fits in, right? It fits in with the theory that the killer could have slipped out the back door and locked it and thrown the bloody shirt into the truck? Since the back is way more private. *If* the killer had a key." What I really wanted was for him to tell me I was wrong. "That seems likely, right?

Now that we know the blood on the shirt was for sure Eloise's?"

Andy stared at me. "Yes, *we* do know that about the blood. But how do *you* know that?"

"Rum punch special. Papa's Seafood. It seems that makes people talk, including evidence technicians."

I would take Andy there to Papa's once this case was put to bed. If anyone could use a rum punch special, it was my man Andy.

"Are you even kidding me?" Andy buried his head in his hands. Then he sat back up. "Hey, listen, Rue. I do appreciate you coming here to tell me about this information. This has been a tremendous help, really solid information. The chief will want someone to have a talk with Dennis right away—and get our hands on those keys."

I scrambled through the jumble in my purse and held them up.

He stared at me again. "You took it upon yourself, Rue, to secure the keys?"

"I am taking it upon myself to let Laurel in the store. Laurel needs her purse, which is currently locked up inside Olde World Treasures."

Andy hesitated. "Well, I technically should take them from you now. They are potential evidence. But can you bring them back? Like, ASAP?"

I stood. "Be back in a jiff." I did want to hurry for my own sake as well. I had to make sure I was home when the sedation started wearing off.

As I said, I was a wimp.

As I walked back to my car, I passed Frannie's Frames and I had a thought. Since Laurel seemed to be in such a rush, I could run into the shop for her since I was already there. Hadn't she said she needed to get something from the frame shop before she got out of town? Surely it was this one. Frannie had long been close with both Eloise and Greta, almost an honorary Endicott.

I stepped into the shop, admiring the oil paintings on the wall that showed off some of the more upscale framing options.

"Hey, good to see you, Rue." Frannie looked up from a picture she was framing. Her gray hair was pulled back into a tight bun, and her trademark red-rimmed glasses were perched low on her nose.

"You doing okay, Frannie? I'm trying to help Laurel get packed up and gone, and I think you might have something for her?"

Frannie's eyes lit up. "Oh, yes! And I love how it turned out. Want to take a look before I wrap it up?"

Curious, I followed her to a long table in the back. There, in a simple oak frame, was the map of Snapdragon Lane. For the second time that day, I felt a chill. Here it was, the map that Laurel told me—in no uncertain terms—she had never seen. The "missing" map she led me to believe the cousins were all still fighting for. Or at least they were fighting for the map that had been on top of this one.

Yet Laurel, it seemed, had known exactly where it was all along, and she planned to take it home. She had pulled some crazy stuff when we were young, but she had been honest always—almost to a fault. The truths she had blurted out had gotten us in trouble more than once.

"Don't you know that this one has a story?" Frannie's voice was filled with admiration. "All of it hand-painted, and it...almost looks like the Endicott homeplace." She stood back to look at it more closely. "I believe it is."

It was a gorgeous map, done in watercolors. Even in my shock, it wasn't lost on me that Eloise's grandfather had been extremely talented. I marveled for a moment at how old it must be. It was a backyard scene with the sea in the distance and red maples scattered among towering black oaks. I could see the gold coin that marked the "pirate treasure" and the dainty little teacup in the spot where Eloise had played with her dolls. A grinning leprechaun danced, half hidden, behind a patch of bright purple blossoms.

"Very nice," I managed.

"Eloise taught all of us a map can be a treasure." Frannie carefully wrapped brown paper around the art to protect it. "Oh, and there's one more thing for Laurel." Moving to the end of the table, she picked up another package covered in brown paper, which she handed to me. "This is another map—which, oddly, Eloise had placed on top of the other. Laurel asked me to separate the two and put them in matching frames. So she could hang them side by side! Won't that make for a nice memory? In honor of her aunt!"

So she had that one too. When I was hiding in the store that day, she'd let the family believe the Newcastle map was missing.

I closed my eyes and took a breath, trying to put it all in perspective. This was a little crazy, but a map, after all, *was no motive for a murder.* I was thinking nonsense. Maybe the sedation was messing with my head.

Plus, Laurel wasn't even here in Massachusetts the day Eloise was killed. There was the thing with Dennis and the key. And also there was Jared; Jared was a creep with no morals whatsoever.

Still, Andy's words came back to me with a pang.

I'm concerned a major suspect may pull a disappearing act if we don't get some things in place to move in for an arrest.

And there was Laurel's sudden rush to get back home so much sooner than she'd planned.

I honestly woke up hoping I could get out of here today.

"And she's all paid up." Frannie interrupted my dark thoughts. "Here is the receipt."

I glanced at it quickly, and I almost gasped when I saw the date the order was put in. "Wait a minute, Frannie. I don't understand. So Laurel was in town *before* her aunt was killed?"

"Oh, yes, she brought in the maps the morning of the Fling just before we heard the news." Frannie shook her head. "How nice she was in town before…well, before it happened. And that she got to spend that little bit of time with Eloise."

And how very odd she hadn't mentioned it.

CHAPTER THIRTEEN

*T*he effects of the anesthesia were starting to wear off, and this was supposed to be the rest-and-feel-better portion of the whole wisdom-teeth ordeal. But red flags were going up—like, almost *glowing* red. Involving both my dentist *and* my childhood friend.

I didn't feel prepared for the confrontation as I drove to Olde World Treasures with the keys for Laurel and the maps she had secretly procured—maps that might or might not be connected to a murder.

She was waiting outside on a bench in white jeans and a pink jean jacket, scrolling through her phone. Her makeup was perfectly applied. She was dressed to hit the road.

Her face lit up when she saw me, and she jumped up off the bench as I got out of my car. "Rue! You've saved

129

my life! Aunt Greta is still napping, if you can believe it. I think it's all just worn her out. All of the company, you know." She gave me a sad smile. "Plus, the way the apartment and the store just don't seem right at all—without Aunt Eloise shuffling around with her cups of tea."

She rattled on enough that I don't think she noticed how unenthusiastically I returned her hug.

With no time for chitchat, I folded my hands across my chest. "I tried to save your life even more by running by the frame shop, like you mentioned in your text." I gave her a look.

Laurel's face went white, and it was a while before she spoke. "Oh, Rue."

"I have your maps in the car. The one you said you'd never seen. And the one you claimed the cousins were all still fighting over."

There was only silence where there should have been some kind of explanation. So I spoke again. "Laurel, what the heck?"

She collapsed onto the bench and put her head in her hands. "It's all so complicated. This *family's* complicated. And the maps belonged to me! I swear! I swear I only took the maps Aunt Eloise had told me she wanted me to have." She looked up at me with pleading eyes. "We talked about it all the time—all the little details about the places on the maps that would belong to me one day." She stared down at the sidewalk. "Like she showed me on the map where she kissed a man she met on a tour—a man she still thought about from her Newcastle trip. And she told me, Rue, I should take my own trip to England, an adventure of my own. Then she made me promise I would go to that place—exactly to that spot. She wanted me to make a wish that I would meet a man like that. And not walk away from him like she did." She nervously ran a hand through her long hair. "We talked about it all the time: where I should go and what I should do by following the map to all her favorite places in Newcastle. How her grandfather's map—that memory of her childhood—would be mine one day. How could I not take them—my aunt's last gift to me?" She paused. "And with the cousins being like they are... I couldn't breathe a word. It was the only way."

It did make a kind of sense. "But you lied to me!" I said.

"I know, and I hated that. I did! But I couldn't take a chance someone would overhear." She let out a sigh. "And how really *stupid* of me to take the maps to Frannie's and not have them framed at home." She wiped away a tear. "But Aunt Eloise used to tell me all the time that part of the magic of the maps came from Frannie's frames."

I wanted to believe her, and I *did* believe her; I sensed

this was the truth. This was Laurel after all. Of course, there was that other lie—about when she arrived in town.

Laurel's voice grew soft. "The last thing she ever said to me was about the Newcastle map and the trip she wanted me to take. 'Throw a lucky penny for me over the Tyne Bridge, and touch the place on the map when you return home to the States,' she said."

"Yeah, how could you not take the maps?" I sat down on the bench beside her.

"It was six months ago that she told me that. We talked about "our" map for about the zillionth time. We looked at it together on the wall behind the register where she used to keep it only for display—with a sign to tell the customers it was not for sale. Then she walked me out of the store and kissed me on the cheek."

There it was again, that chill. "And you never saw Eloise again?"

Laurel shook her head. "It's hard to get back to town with my crazy schedule—although I should have made the effort."

"But that's another lie." I looked her in the eye and wondered how well I'd really known her over all these years. "Laurel, you were here. You were at Frannie's Frames on the very morning Eloise was killed."

A look of alarm passed through Laurel's eyes, and

she took a breath. "Oh, Rue. You don't understand," she said in a frightened whisper. "This is all…just a mess."

I gave her a hard look. "Make me understand."

She looked up and down the street to make sure we were alone. "Okay, I was here. I came here to get the maps. Not to *steal* the maps, because I would never do that. I came here to the store the day before the murder, and that's when Aunt Eloise *handed* them to me. Out of her own free will. She said it was time that I took them home. I was doing nothing wrong!"

"Okay, I still don't get it. Why all the secrecy? She wasn't handing you some artifacts worth a million dollars. *What exactly is the deal?* Why did everybody want that one map of some place in England when there *were so many maps?*"

"My aunt used to tease me about the pirate treasure, and Jared must have overheard and gotten the idea that she was giving me some zillion-dollar piece of art. Like, she used to wink at me, and say, 'When that map makes you rich, you can have your own show like the Car-crash-ians.' That was how she said their names—you know, the Kardashians. To her it was a joke. But I guess he thought she meant the map was really worth a lot. And then all the other cousins must have thought so too. Because I guess that goofy Jared spread his igno-rance around." She looked up at me. "I *had* to keep it quiet, that I had the maps. Because Jared scares me, Rue."

"Like, what do you think he would do?"

"I'd like to think he wouldn't hurt me, my own cousin, but I wouldn't put it past him to kind of rough me up to get his hands on that map. He had no idea, of course, there were *two* maps in the frame. And he didn't care about the Newcastle map; he just cared about the money. And I think he suspected she gave it to me that day."

"Why do you think that?"

"I went out that night with my mother for a drink, and, Rue, there he was, in the back of the bar—just staring. My mom waved at him, all happy, not even noticing he was *creeping* on me. Then he came over to the table and asked me where was the map."

"And what did you say?"

"I told him it was mine, that Aunt Eloise had promised and he should go the heck away. But then, Rue, I lied. I said I didn't have it yet, so he could quit his spying. I figured that would give me time to get out of town before he could figure out I lied."

"But the day after that…"

Both of us were silent.

I asked her quietly, "If Jared thought the maps were

still in the store—and that you would take them soon—
do you think it's possible that Jared..."

Laurel's eyes grew wide. "You don't think that he
broke into the store to get them and that my cousin..."
She paused. "I worried he would hurt me—but not that
he would *kill* me. Jared is a jerk, but surely..."

What had my parrot said not long after the murder?
Little bits of gossip he had overheard:

Watch out for family.

Greed will get you every time.

*The ones that you keep close are the ones to break your
heart.*

Jared already had it in his head that getting Eloise
out of the picture could get the shop on the market and
speed up his inheritance. And now he might have
thought he could grab a map to make him next-level
rich.

Had Zeke just overheard some idle gossip? Or had
that day-after talk been coming from someone who
knew?

CHAPTER FOURTEEN

$\mathcal{M}$y jaw was throbbing at that point, so I set off to take the keys to Andy—along with even more information for him. (At that point, I thought I deserved a badge.) Then I would find an ice pack and my pillow and let him do his job.

I held up a hand in goodbye as Laurel's BMW disappeared around the curve. Then I turned back to the store where Eloise would never again greet me with her warm smile and a "Darling, come on in."

I stared at the doors and the overflowing concrete planters, silent witnesses that had seen the killer come and go. If only they could talk, I thought. But mayflowers tell no tales. Frustrated, I walked back and forth in front of the doors—as if I could somehow soak up some kind of vision of whatever evil had visited the space.

And that is when I saw it: a small piece of bright blue and green plastic wedged behind one of the pots. It was one of those little spinning toys. When I leaned forward to pick it up, I noticed it was blue and green and *red.* As in, speckles of red blood—a whole lot of blood.

Feeling breathless with the knowledge of what that had to mean, I straightened up to leave the little object in place for the cops. I was not about to mess up the chain of evidence; I knew all about that stuff from Andy (and my favorite thriller authors).

And so I headed back to Prestige Investigations, full of information and with a sinking heart.

Ten minutes later, as I entered Andy's office, I could hear him on the phone again. He had the kind of tone that meant things in his world were happening at lightning speed—and I knew the feeling well; it was that kind of day all around.

I sat down in his office till he got off the phone.

Then I pushed the keys across his desk as promised. "Andy! It was Dennis! He for sure was the one who killed Eloise." My heart was pounding against my chest, and I was feeling breathless. "I was just at the antique shop, and you won't believe what—"

Andy grabbed the keys. "Well, I hate to say it, but Rue, we feel the same. Dennis was the one who had the opportunity to slip in and out unnoticed." He paused and gave me a sad look. "Dennis had financial motive. And the fingerprints on the sword came back to Dennis too. These keys that you've found have almost sealed the deal. And Rue, I'm truly grateful—and impressed." He let out a sigh. "But they're telling us we need more to get a warrant."

"But—" I could not interrupt too forcefully. My mouth hurt too much, and Andy was wound up.

"The prints, on one hand," he said, "are a nice piece of evidence. But on the other hand, Dennis spent a lot of time in the antique shop, and it was common knowledge that he loved to pick up a sword from time to time to study it a bit. A lot of us like the swords."

"Andy, it was him! Without a doubt. Because I just discovered—"

"And it's become somewhat urgent we make an arrest *right now*. Because we've become aware that Dennis has an airline ticket to Chicago—a one-way ticket, Rue. He's in a lot of debt, we've learned. So it would not make sense for him to plunk down a pile of money on some big vacation when he can't even pay his bills. But if he feels the need to run? Well, in that case, a man would spend whatever money it might take to get himself out of town, and quickly."

"Well, then it's super lucky that just now I found—"

"And even now our suspect might have his bags all packed. We need just one more piece of evidence, and we need it fast."

"Like something that belonged to Dennis? And was found behind a planter at the entrance to the shop—with blood all spattered on it?"

He looked at me, astonished. "What are you telling me?"

"Well, as I said before, I've just come from the antique shop." Then I went on to describe to Andy my startling discovery.

He stood up from his desk. "First the keys, then this. Rue, how do you do it?" Without waiting for an answer, he grabbed for his phone. "If you will excuse me, we'll need to run with this—ASAP."

It still seemed surreal. "I still can't believe it, Andy. I was just in his office! He just took out some of my teeth!"

"Which was lucky for all." In his rush to get things

going, he paused to meet my eye. "You go home and get some rest. And thank you, Rue. Good job."

Two days later, things were somewhat back to normal. I pointed a tall boy with glasses to the shelf where he could find the store's last copy of *The Alchemist*. He would also find a coupon tucked inside since that was the final book to be discovered on our literary treasure hunt. This kid must have recognized the sycamore tree growing out of the ruins of a church as being from the classic book. I saw him grin from ear to ear when he found the coupon, good for two hundred dollars' worth of food from Papa's Seafood.

I texted Melanie. "The treasure hunt has officially come to a conclusion," I typed in. "Let's do it again sometime."

I got back a thumbs-up.

The store had been busy with people coming in to talk about the arrest. Andy had come by the night before with ice cream to fill in some more details. Dennis, knowing Eloise had plans to close the shop to work at the Spring Fling, had plotted out a scheme to take the sword, some pricey figurines, and some antique jewelry, which he planned to stuff into a garbage bag. That way, if someone saw him out behind the store, it would look as if he were going to the dumpster shared by his florist shop and Eloise's and several other businesses.

Eloise, however, had forgotten all about the Fling and surprised Dennis in the store just as he reached for the sword. With expensive items stuffed into a bag beside him, it was clear why he was in the store.

"And he just panicked, Rue," said Andy. "I don't believe I've ever seen that much remorse in a suspect. He was just beside himself." Andy shook his head. "He's basically a good man. Who in the worst moment of his life did an evil thing. Which he instantly regretted."

"Eloise and Greta were very good to him," I said. "It just hurts my heart."

After exiting, Dennis had thrown his bloody shirt into the back of the truck Barney used for his deliveries. He had a change of clothes waiting at the florist shop, which had not yet opened for the day. Then, looking fresh and clean, he had headed to the Fling.

"Somewhere in the process, he lost that little fidget toy—which was his undoing." Andy licked at his Rocky Road. "He knew that it likely had blood spattered on it, and he knew his staff and patients would recognize that it was his. A lot of people knew those little toys are kind of a thing with him." He leaned back in his chair as Ollie climbed up into his lap. "So he walked back and forth a few times in front of the antique shop in the days following the murder, hoping he could find it. He could not go *in* the shop, because Greta closed it up for a few days."

I took a careful bite of my ice cream—lemon custard—and I had a thought. "*That's* what was up with him when I saw him in town that day. Because he told me he was going to the florist's. Then he went the other way."

"It's interesting," said Andy. "There are still some items missing that were taken from the store. It took them a while, but the family had finally come up with a list just before we arrested Dennis. We found some things in his home, but he swore up and down that was all he took." Andy leaned back in his chair. "And I tend to believe him. Why admit to a brutal murder and not admit to all of the stuff you stole?"

I thought for a moment. "Andy, have you looked at Laurel's cousin Jared?" I explained about Jared's greed and his horrible behavior. He would not have been above swiping items from his aunts' shop to raise some money for himself.

"Yeah, we had our eye on him during our investigation. Because Jared has a record, mainly petty thefts. But you've hit on something, Rue. Just because we cleared the guy for murder doesn't mean he didn't swipe that missing stuff."

Ollie let out a meow and jumped off Andy's lap. Then my small furry friend returned to the Gatsby-Beasley-Ollie pile snuggled up against my leg. The three of them had been sticking close to me since I came home after my procedure. Great nurses, every one.

Now, as I straightened a display in the store, the parrot suddenly sang out, startling a woman who was browsing in the thriller section.

"The dentist did it!" squawked the parrot. "Safe to walk the streets again! Killed in her own shop!" (Zeke sometimes liked to talk in bursts.)

"This bird isn't boosting our town's reputation," I told Elizabeth, trying not to laugh. "I hope he doesn't scare the tourists."

Elizabeth shot me a grin. "The chamber of commerce, I imagine, is not a fan of Zeke."

My phone dinged with a text, and I looked down to see it was from Andy. "We searched Jared's house and found the missing items."

I sent him a thumbs-up emoji. I knew that guy was up to something.

Happy with the news that Jared hadn't gotten away with his theft, I straightened up the gift sets of book-plates. "Do you know what I think I'll do when I get off from work?" I said to Elizabeth. "I want to go to Greta's and buy myself a map." I wanted a little of that magic from my childhood to hang up in my den. Maybe I would buy a map of a place I'd like to one day go so I could dream and plan while I sat and looked at it.

Or maybe I'd get a map of some ancient place with older dreams from another time, dreams preserved in ink and imagination.

I wanted for myself a little paper world of possibilities—or ghosts—to put in a gold frame.

"I think I'll go with you," said Elizabeth. "I might get a map as well." She brushed some hair out of her eyes. "Hey, I heard that Greta has decided she won't sell the shop. And she's made it final. She's already lost her sister, and Somerset Harbor, she says, feels like her other family. She doesn't want to lose us too."

"I was hoping she'd decide that. She can help us choose our maps."

And maybe after work I would take a walk in my favorite little park. There were always ducks swimming in the lake and a whole parade of people walking with their dogs or throwing frisbees. I would walk and *look*. Because Eloise had taught me to always look for stories.

I loved the stories that I sold, the kinds that filled my shelves. But there are stories *outside* books, stories everywhere that play out for the smart ones—and the lucky ones—who take the time to see.

As was taught to me by a special friend—the grand lady of the maps.

# # #

Thank you for reading! Want to help out?

Reviews are crucial for independent authors like me, so if you enjoyed my book, **please consider leaving a review today**.

Thank you!

Penny Brooke

ABOUT THE AUTHOR

Penny Brooke has been reading mysteries for as long as she can remember. When not penning her own stories, she enjoys spending time outdoors with her husband, crocheting, and cozying up with her pups and a good novel. To find out more about her books, visit www.pennybrooke.com

Made in United States
Orlando, FL
04 May 2023